HURDLES

by

Suzanne Wetanson

For my sister Laurie

It is my belief that the greatest gift a person can give oneself is to create a passion. be it art, music, sports, writing - anything, where you can lose yourself; where action is effortless, without conscious thought and your inner-self takes over. This is complete freedom. Time is meaningless. You have no borders.

My passion is sculpture. To chip away at a block of marble until my envisioned image emerges is thrilling. Writing too, the words fall into place and weave the story.

I used to ride horses. Artwork is safer.

Acknowledgements

To open I'd like to express my gratitude for the COVER – art/design by JOE CHIERCHIO, which he created for me with love.

Thank you, thank you to Ken Neill whose computer expertise saved me from tearing out my hair many times. Many times.

And of course my children. Their excitement to hear what would happen in the next chapter spurred me on and made the writing even more fun.

I
SCORPIO

CHAPTER 1

Muscles taut. Senses sharp. Waiting. Waiting. Waiting.

She stood alone on the hilltop peering through the early morning mist beyond the meadow into the Fall spectrum of the bordering woodland. A cold snap. Autumn had come late to South Carolina, well into October. People of Charleston were used to dramatic climate changes

God, it was quiet, peaceful in contrast to her anticipation. She pulled on her white turtleneck sweater. Waiting. A moment...now, yes. At once, there was a change in the atmosphere. She straightened, straining her ears and eyes.

Suddenly, a far off rumbling. There...bursting from the East, a vibrant image approaching rapidly. She rubbed her eyes and squinted toward the sun. The rumbling became a cacophony of barking dogs and pounding hooves. Lathered horses tense with pursuit, snorting through flared nostrils, breathed steam into the cold air veiling their riders. It was the Classic Hunt. At the head, amid a pack of Beagle Hounds goaded by their inbred lust for the chase, was John Hamil - The Master, sounding the bugle, resplendent in his coat of flaming red. His powerful dappled gray Hunter jumped the stream followed by the other riders. There must have been more than thirty. Water splashed from the horses' hooves as an eruption of diamonds. Raw and thrilling was the display of the Hunter and the Hunted in the predatory order of survival and she knew one day she would be part of it.

Hamil rode into the woods. She could see his coat flash among the trees, the members of the Hunt galloping behind him. Then, all was gone from sight. The rumbling. Silence.

There was perspiration on her forehead. It was an exhilaration she hadn't experienced in all her twenty-eight years. She reminded herself that the correct term for the Master's coat was 'Pink' and smiled at the irony. Marisa Rait was not one to be swayed by words. *Pink?* There was nothing 'Pink' about a foxhunt; it was hot and frenzied as any pagan blood ritual.

***

Being Sunday, Marisa adhered to the manners of her rigid "Blue Blood" upbringing, gritted her teeth and waited until after three o'clock, a proper time, to call Hamil Farm. She was nervous, and though alone in her house, closed the door to the bedroom while she dialed.

"Hello." Said a woman's pleasant voice.

"John Hamil, please."

"I'm sorry, my husband is giving a lesson now. Who's calling?"

The strong accent was unfamiliar. Marisa gave her name.

"One moment, I will get a pencil."

The receiver was put down and Marisa heard fading footsteps. It never occurred to her that he was married. Her vision of John Hamil was a romantic figure riding out from a bygone era of gallantry into the twenty-first century. She couldn't think of him as an ordinary man with a family and a business to run.

Growing up, Marisa had submerged herself in the world of books and movies where anything was possible; failure was only an incentive for greater effort and success its just reward. In fantasy she was able to escape her mother's endless 'dos and don'ts' as she poked into her life while dashing to The Ladies Garden Club or The Charleston Yacht Club, leaving Marisa alone with a succession of nannies. Dutifully, she suffered her mother's insistence that her daughter have a proper cotillion and 'come out' as a debutante according to the social code of Southern old-moneyed families. Her father gave her what little time he could which was rare and only on weekends because the stock market and banks were closed. She adored her father, trusted his love, and knew he felt sorry for her, his only child, so lonely in the big house downtown in

The Battery, which had been his family home for generations.

Sidney Lawner was an aristocrat; so was his wife, Frances. They had been children together, and at nineteen years old were wed as expected. They were fond of one another, respected one another and probably grew to love one another in a dispassionate way that Marisa found personally intolerable. They were fair, watercolor people. Surely, somewhere in the family there must have been a renegade. She brushed out her black hair that fell in waves to her shoulders and regarded the freckles that still dotted her nose. How her mother frowned at those blemishes from beneath raised eyebrows and the wide brim hat she always wore to protect her creamy Magnolia skin, which she professed, was the prize of any decent Southern lady. Yes, Marisa was certain, she was the renegade. Her father? There was never a time that his patience and understanding of her childhood dilemmas were lacking or his advice withheld. She did however realize that to be a child with a single parent, for virtually that is what she was, put too much responsibility on each of them. Happily, at twenty years old, she fell in love and married Warren Rait.

They met at her father's annual Christmas party for his business associates. Boring though it was Warren was there because as a builder it was important to maintain a warm relationship with prospective investors. Marisa was there because she had run out of excuses not to come and her father had insisted sternly, lovingly.

Marisa was occupying her time helping her mother ladle eggnog from the giant crystal bowl surrounded by white sugary macaroons and a traditional fruit cake that no one ever touched when Warren stepped up to the table. He introduced himself as she filled his cup. She saw her mother smile; appearances were her measure of acceptance and Warren had her full attention,

Standing tall as her father, Warren had a defiant chin softened by a trimmed three day's growth of a dark beard which Marisa found herself wanting to touch. His eyes gave warning that he knew what she was thinking. This ability, she supposed, was acquired from early training. It made her uncomfortable but along with a disarming manner and a gentle voice he intrigued her and she returned his gaze with matched impudence.

Warren, ten years her senior, was an established real-estate investor/builder and *'quite comfortable financially'*, much to the relief of her parents. Now, eight years later, Warren remained her safe-haven, her one and only lover.

A rustle; the woman picked up the receiver breaking her reverie. "Rait did you say; R-A-I-T, is that correct?"

"Yes. I'd like to make an appointment for lessons."

"Of course. Ah...can you come tomorrow morning at ten o'clock? He'll be able to meet you and evaluate your riding skills. Then he can fit you into a class."

"Does Mr. Hamil give private lessons?"

"Yes. Yes, he does. If you come tomorrow, you will be able to speak with him."

"I'll be there at ten. Can you give me directions from Charleston?" She wrote quickly, estimating a two-hour trip northward to Camden, not far from where she had watched the Hunt yesterday. "Thank-you, good-bye."

"Good-bye." Mrs. Hamil said gently.

The next moment Marisa was rummaging in her closet, digging out her old boots and breeches. She hadn't used them since her father gave up riding for golf ten years ago at his wife's insistence. Together they used to gallop and play hide-and-seek among the towering Oak trees, then chase each other up to the high ground. Those trees, with their canopies draped in moss, created an air of mystery to the heavy stillness. Oh, what high adventure it was to be with her father.

She thought of telling Warren about her plans and the excitement the Hunt had stirred in her, but decided against it. Lately, he was too busy, always too busy with his real estate acquisitions, to say more than: '*That's nice, Darling.*' He would placate her, figuring it was just another of her all-consuming endeavors like writing her novel or perfecting her tennis game or taking the job as a newspaper reporter. *It would pass.*

But five years later she was still working for The Charleston Post and her most exciting item was the birth of triplets last year. It was a local tabloid; Charlestonians were loyal and picked it up weekly. Rob MacGrath was proud of that, he started the paper thirty years ago and was a celebrity in town. MacGrath covered the big stories – Charleston and vicinity had its share of robberies, fraud and violence, instinctively Mac exposed the core of the matter. Last Friday morning his handsome face looked troubled; Marisa was surprised when he stopped at her desk.

"Marisa there's been another accident out at Hamil Farm; that's four this year. Something fishy is going on there, I'm sure of it."

Marisa liked hearing him speak; his Scottish heritage could not be clearer if he were wearing a kilt.

"You're a rider and I don't doubt you know men, see what you can find out."

"Warren." Marisa attempted to reach him. Of all the people in the world, she wanted to share her life with her husband.

He was rustling through his papers. "Yes, Darling." They stared at each other awkwardly.

"I'm going to Hamil Farm for a riding lesson today, maybe you could meet me there later. It's not far from *Raittown"*.

"Marisa, I have a meeting with the zoning board. Have fun, I won't be late tonight." He kissed her cheek, snapped closed his briefcase, and was gone.

13

Had he looked over his shoulder, he would have seen the sadness and hurt in her face, but Marisa knew that he was off with no more thought to her than to yesterday's corn bread. It wasn't enough that Warren loved her. "Recognize me," Her heart shouted.

Warren wanted a baby. All talk ended in the same confrontation: "Marisa, isn't it time we started a family?" But Warren was no longer her soulmate, though she yearned for him. She found she had made the mistake of hastily exchanging one lonely life for another. She wouldn't bring a child into a world of loneliness. Experience told her that a child needs two parents to love and feel loved and have time to develop without being a burden to one and responsible for the other.

He had left her with an empty heart, feeling invisible to her husband not knowing how to reach him emotionally or physically - they were separated. In bed, when she touched him he shrugged her away as he would a fly.

During their marriage, in the seclusion of their bedroom, they shared dreams and fears. She believed she knew Warren. They were similar people. Warren was an only child like she was in practicality and like herself, he idolized his father who was his sole source of guidance, support and comfort. His mother, he told her, had died when he was too young to remember. It was their backgrounds that differed. Marisa's parents were both college graduates. Warren's father was a plumber, however he refused to go to school for a license. He maintained a lucrative business by hiring others ro dirty their hands while he negotiated "big deals" with building contractors. Warren had never known his father to lose a deal and from him learned the mastery and secret of success: *defeat is intolerable.*

When Warren started college his father gave him what he called "the gift of a lifetime". He said. "There are those who study books. I study people – an education far more valuable and not available in books. Remember, know well whom you are dealing with - their friends, their enemies and their most treasured possessions."

His father died before graduation, before the lawyers told him he was adopted. In fits of shock, and anger Warren grieved the loss of his father. The pain didn't subside, with time it lodged in a place where he learned to live with it leaving a scar of fury. And he grieved the loss of his identity. He was a man ravished of all he believed in, a man without lineage. He saw himself as a lone lion roaming the jungle prepared to create and protect his own Pride at any cost, and he would mark his territory. First he dissolved his father's plumbing business and used his inheritance to build a low cost housing development he named "Raittown" Today five "Raittowns" dot Charleston and vicinity, and the name Warren Rait is well respected in the financial world and southern society.

All this Marisa knew but found lineage a selfish excuse for having a child; if she had a baby they would share the joy of parenting.

***

It was the quiet time, the waiting time, when the sun's first light appeared, bathing the pasture and bordering woodlands in a warm glow. Last night's rain had been heavy; mist rose from the wet ground. The man was barely discernible as he moved about the paddocks and entered the turreted barn. The awakened horses made soft muttering sounds. He had been in this country for seventeen years. Each morning he walked with pride about his twenty-acre farm of spreading fields and corrals of Hunters and champion jumpers, renewing his satisfaction in the prestigious position he held in the equestrian community. By ten o'clock he was ready to instruct his class of intermediate riders.

The morning was clear and cold. Once on the freeway, Marisa relaxed and enjoyed the drive. The urban scene merged into the greenery of the rural countryside, leaving behind the string of islands connected to each other by long, tall bridges. Charleston was a peninsula below sea level on the Atlantic Ocean between the Ashley River and Cooper River. The many islands were mostly summer communities so the traffic was lighter now than during the Spring up until after Labor Day. She passed signs to the Wateree River, where she and Warren had often gone for picnics and fishing. Kershaw County was so much lusher than Charleston, and exhibited the changing seasons flagrantly. Following directions, she turned off the Interstate; fifteen minutes later she, at last, saw the small hand lettered plaque by the side of the wooded road. *Hamil Farm.*

The Jeep sloshed along the lane worn into gullies filled with rainwater. The road wound past a number of split-rail fenced corrals where a few horses grazed. A Bay trotted forward and bellowed a high-pitched whinny in greeting, while the others raised their heads from bales of hay to fix her with an inquisitive eye. To the left was a modest white farmhouse built within a grove of Oak Trees to shelter it from the fierce heat of summer.

A door slammed. A little girl, her blonde corn silk braids bobbing on her shoulders, ran off the porch.

"Bye, Mama. I have to hurry."
"Rose-Marie, don't go through the woods today; you'll get all wet."

"It's okay, Mama. If I go this way, I won't be late for math." Called the child putting on a navy blazer over the plaid skirt of a parochial school uniform. "Papa gave Cinnamon and me a special lesson." She would rather risk a failing grade and suffer the harsh punishment of The Sisters than come under her father's disappointed gaze. Her knees were already sore from kneeling motionless for hours on the cement floor of the chapel. "It's all right, Mama, really." Her blue eyes sparkled with mischief, and Marisa readily recognized her own fierce spirit in the delicate girl.

Even from a distance she was able to see the mother's shoulders slump in defeat. She remained

17

on the porch until the child was out of sight, then wiped her hands on her housedress and went back inside the house. The Sisters had called her often to arrange a conference with the teachers but her English was not practiced enough for her to understand, and she would be embarrassed. She wished her husband would take the time, but he said he paid the bills; it's their job to handle the discipline of the students. Eventually they stopped calling.

Marisa drove around the bend, and caught a glimpse of bed sheets flying on the clothesline in the yard behind the veranda. In a world dependent on mechanical conveniences it was refreshing to see clothes drying in the sunlight; not many women did hand laundry these days.

Further on were two small barns and a long bui lding with high windows. The road came to an abrupt end in front of a huge circular barn. Actually, she realized, there were a series of barns dominated by a turret-shaped roof. All the structures showed sunbleached traces of moss green paint. Topping the turret was a weather vane with a golden horse, its mane and tail flying as it galloped after the wind. It was the shimmering horse that had caught her attention from the country road.

Marisa parked in the designated area. There were no other cars or people in sight. She saw she was overlooking a large meadow onto which the night rain was running in rivulets. It was empty except for white pole stances, and a high stack of tree trunks in the far corner - a jump course.

Like a fool she had not asked where to meet John Hamil. With no better alternative, she walked up the gradual incline to the entrance of the main barn. Its giant doors minified her in the opening. As she entered, Marisa was aware of the same awesome reverence that engulfed her when her father had taken her into St. Patrick's Cathedral in New York City. Instead of ghostly organ music, the cavernous barn was filled with the low-pitched resonance of steady, genial munching. Sunlight streamed in through the door silvering the floating bits of sawdust in the semi-darkness.

"Mr. Hamil?" She called softly, and waited. It was just ten o'clock. She stepped further into the gloaming. "Mr. Hamil, its Marisa Rait."

"I be there." A low voice of the indistinct accent replied.

She sighed in relief.

A man leading a dark horse, came from the left side aisle. He was dressed in brown and blended into the surroundings with a similarity only acquired by constant proximity. She waited for him to introduce himself. His appearance didn't measure up to the man she had seen charging among the hounds or the remarkable stories she had heard of the great equestrian. He was of average height and slightly built, but for the saddle muscles that swelled in his breeches above the high topped boots. Neither were his features prominent, only his light eyes, which shone with brilliance beneath his weather-sworn brown hat.

"I'm John Hamil." He touched the brim of his hat and inclined his head, and Marisa, on verification of his identity, was disappointed.

She thought he would remove his glove and shake her hand, which she extended to him, but he ignored the gesture. He hooked a lead line from the left side of the horse's halter to the wall and did the same to the right side; thus the animal was stationary in the center of the aisle. He handed Marisa two brushes. "His name is Scorpio. You brush him each time before you saddle him." He demonstrated with strong, sweeping motions. Although his diction was inaccurate, he spoke English unfalteringly, as if he had been doing so for many years.

"When you finish, we get the tack. I show you how you will saddle the horse, then you show me how you ride him. Stand next to me."

He made it look effortless, but when Marisa tried to tighten the girth she needed help. He reached under the horse's belly, took the strap falling from the side of the saddle and using two hands, yanked upward, fastening the cinch. She did it. The next task was to place the bit in Scorpio's mouth, which he stubbornly refused to open. There, too, was a trick.

Hamil demonstrated. "Put your fingers to the back of his jaw, here, behind the teeth. He opens his mouth." With the other hand he slid the bit in and pulled the bridle over the horse's head. "The ears go through here. Then, loosely buckle the cheek pieces." He inserted two fingers to demonstrate the tautness desired.

Marisa opened the buckles and closed them again.

"You got it." He unsnapped the lead lines; they fell to the floor with a clink. "Take him to the indoor ring - over there." He waved an arm. "We work inside today. Grass is too slippery on the lower ground." Hamil said, handing Marisa the reins and indicating the curious long building. "The intermediate class has a lesson there in half an hour. You do the flat work with them; watch the jumping. After, we talk." John Hamil spoke with unquestionable authority. His instructions, she interpreted as orders. His aura of power returned.

He turned and walked down the aisle into the maze of stalls. Marisa stood alone with Scorpio. The horse sniffed her for his own evaluation and stood patiently. The munching continued. Ten horses lounged elegantly in oversized plush stalls. Outside of each was a polished brass nameplate: Hamil's *Hero, Hamil's Prince, Hamil's Gold, Hamil's..., Hamil's..., Hamil's....* These were his prize exhibitors. The back barns, were for borders and lesson horses.

Marisa led Scorpio outside into the sunshine. Six cars were now in the parking area. A young woman, about her own age, gingerly pulled a saddle from the tailgate of a station wagon as Marisa passed on the way to the indoor ring.

"Good morning." Marisa greeted, but the girl stared at her emptily, and hurried inside the barn.

'Friendly sort,' Marisa thought sourly, looking after her. She walked Scorpio through the narrow door to the indoor ring.

CHAPTER 2

The indoor arena was even larger than it had appeared. Set up at various intervals on the earthen floor were an assortment of obstacles: a white fence, a number of split log rails, and a low brush-box with an artificial green hedge. The clerestory windows were open for fresh air, and though it was chilly outside, it was comfortable to ride in shirtsleeves. Eight riders were in various stages of preparation for the lesson. A blond lady on a gray was cantering around the perimeter. Marisa supposed the horse was an Arab, what with its small head, long mane, and flowing tail; he was closer coupled than the others and resembled a rocking horse as he loped along. A middle-aged gentleman, Marisa had heard addressed as 'Your Honor,' helped a lady, probably his wife, to mount. The two walked their horses before breaking into a trot. No one acknowledged Marisa. The girl from the station wagon was astride a large black gelding, adjusting her stirrups.

Eight riders were lining up.
"Walk."

Marisa turned to see the instructor leaning on the stile near the door; a mangy German Shepherd at his feet.

"Mrs. Rait, I give you a knee up." She bent her left knee, held onto the saddle as the Judge's wife had done, and he boosted her to the seat. He adjusted her stirrups and checked the girth. "Walk and show me how you do in the other gaits."

Marisa guided Scorpio to a place behind the line.

"Trot now."
Scorpio trotted smoothly at the command. Posting to a trot, like riding a bicycle, once learned, becomes instinctual. She hadn't forgotten.

"Canter." A sharp command.
Scorpio obeyed.

She tightened her knees around the horse's flank.

"Standing position. Mrs. Rait, stand in the stirrups; get off the withers, keep your heels down. Chin up, eyes front, look between his ears. Loosen up on his mouth." The commands came in a staccato fashion. "You got it. Faster. Full canter."

The blond woman in the lead quickened the pace. Marisa had never felt so free. It was effortless, as if she were sailing and the animal was free of her weight.

"Ho." And Scorpio did, on the spot. Had it not been for the vise-like grip of her knees, Marisa would have been sent flying over his head.

"We go the other way."

Marisa was now in the lead. They walked for a few minutes.

"Trot on."

They moved out with reaching strides. A huge rat scurried from the corner, just avoided Scorpio's flying hooves, and darted back. On the next lap, Marisa could see its marble, black eyes peeping about avariciously. The brazen creature evacuated its shelter and began scavenging around the heap of sawdust that had accumulated against the wall.

"Canter."

The German Shepherd barked.
She pressed her knees together to signal the horse to change gaits, but he had already heard, and obeyed. John Hamil ruled here.

"Forward position."

Marisa moved her weight forward. This time she was prepared for the eventual 'Ho.'

"We jump now. Mrs. Rait, stay mounted and stand here by the entrance. Watch carefully. The heels are down, knees tight; the rider is in forward position on the approach and over the jump. Watch Vicky, how she follows the action of the horse."

The blond moved out of line toward the center ground.

"We do the In-and-Out, the Three-in--One, come around over the rail, then the coop. Slowly now, Vicky, he likes to speed it up. Let him loose when you turn him into the fence. Go."

Vicky clucked to her horse, trotted a few paces, tightened her knees and the Arab advanced at a slow canter. His silvery mane cascaded behind him. She directed the horse's head slightly to the

outside of the ring.   As they approached the fence
Marisa saw her turn his head squarely to the barrier.
The horse's ears perked up. He jumped the fence,
took one stride, and jumped the slightly higher
second fence, *'In-and-Out'*

"Slow, Vicky, steady now." Hamil
instructed while walking to each fence.

Vicky completed the course, patted her
horse briskly on the neck, and went to the rear of
the line.

"You keep him tightly controlled like that a few
more lessons; we get rid of the martingale for the
Hunt. He be fine. Your Honor…"

He was a short, heavy-set man on a long
legged, thick-barreled Hunter the color of polished
copper. The Judge watched Hamil. At his nod the
big horse did the In-and Out with ease and
approached the Three-In-One. The Judge kicked
him, urging him on and reined his head toward the
jump. The horse snorted, and skidded to a halt
directly in front of the fence. The man lunged
forward, smacking his mouth on the animal's neck,
slid to the side and was barely able to regain his
seat.

Hamil's face betrayed his disgust. "Your
wrists are stiff. Dismount. I take him."

Obediently, the pudgy man dismounted.

Hamil rode the horse faultlessly and
elegantly, over the course. He reined up beside the
man who appeared shrunken with humility. "Take
it again. Dusty!"

The dog sprang forward, snarling and
snapping his teeth behind the frightened 'Shining

Penny'. Blood dribbled down the Judge's chin; he wiped it away with his sleeve and turned his lathered mount into the Three-in-One. They trotted, and then slowly cantered. Bravely, the Judge stuck out his chin and prodded his heels to the horse's flank. Shining Penny took the first fence, two strides, the second fence, a stride and out over the third fence. The Three-in-One completed, they faced the rail and the coop with Dusty frightfully attacking the horse's tail. This time it was a flawless execution. The Judge patted his horse. Dusty returned to sit placidly beside Hamil.

"Next."

The Judge's now shaken wife reined out of the line on a lusterless, vigorless mount.

"Just do the last fence, Mrs. Woodhouse. You be fine. Slow trot."

The woman led her horse to step over the log, which had been lain on the ground. Hamil made no comment. He pointed to the end of the line, having dismissed her as an apparent waste of time. He reset the rail to its original height. "Ellen, how is Fog today? He looked sharp on the trail Saturday."

The girl from the station wagon; Ellen took the In-and-Out, the Three-in-One.
"Good. You doing better."

She attacked the rail and final fence in a flurry; the horse's hoof knocked off the rail.

"Sloppy, sloppy work. Do it all over. If I see that again you don't come back here." He reset the crossbar.

All eyes were riveted on Ellen, who was now ashen and shamefaced. She trotted, then cantered slowly, without error, through the course, retiring to the rear of the line. Marisa looked on with the magnetism of one watching a spider spin its web, trap its prey and let it squirm until he was ready to devour it.

Each rider subsequently took his turn and then again with a slight variation in the jump sequence. After the lesson, the students went wordlessly about their business in the barn. Quite plainly there was no fellowship between these people. Just as plainly they closed their ears without apathy to Hamil's berating and kept strict control not to make eye contact with one another.

Hamil signaled to Marisa to remain. After the last rider left he came and stood beside her. "Mrs. Rait, have you ever jumped?"

"No, but I would like to and I'd like to eventually join the Hunt." She said, realizing that there is more to riding a horse than hopping on his back and dashing away, as she had done with her father. When Rob MacGrath, the paper's editor, gave her this challenging assignment she was prepared to observe. He had told her it would be impossible to interview Hamil forthrightly; the man answered to no one. It turned out to be something more and she was part of it.

It was told that John Hamil was fifty, however his face gave no indication of age, only the level of contempt he held for the meek, and the expectations he had for the stout-hearted. There was a unique kinship between this man and his animals.

He schooled them with an innate understanding. As with his students, the slightest error was punished, remembered and never repeated. Students at Hamil Farm traveled distances to be under his tutelage. All revered him, though some probably despised him. The disciplines he imposed on himself were rigorous; he expected no less from his students. A rider presented with a jump would get over, no question - simple as the Earth. For John Hamil you rode for ribbons or foxes. Ribbons were the proof of his superiority as an instructor. In the Spring the horse shows were held every weekend. All his apprentices were trained for that competition. The theater on the opposite side of the calendar was the Classic Hunt - a remnant of a time long past.

"We try a low rail. Trot around two times, then lead him over this pole." He laid a crossbar from the fence on the ground. "You be in jumping position, keep the reins loose. Scorpio will take you over." He stood by the rail watching her closely Scorpio jumped the rail with ease, giving Marisa self-confidence, though illusionary.

"We do it again at a canter." He reset the crossbar to form an X one-foot from the ground. "Hold the reins as if you held a bird in your hands, gently enough not to crush it, but firmly enough not to let it escape."

It was a lovely adage, spoken in a tone that was gentle as was the message. When she released her knuckle-white grip so did she release her tension and became sensitive to the intellect and ability of the horse. It was a partnership; he waited for her to guide him. She directed Scorpio to the post and pressed him to a canter. Once more came the intoxicating rush of success - the onset of an unquenchable thirst. Hamil watched her go over the obstacle until she mastered the use of her body in time, and position with the horse. She smiled at the teacher with warm gratitude.

"You be in the Hunt by next fall, sure, Mrs. Rait. Join the class on Monday morning. Wednesdays at ten o'clock we do the private lesson. You be fine." Hamil caught her waist as she dismounted.

She felt his breath against her face before she moved away. Marisa didn't believe she was beautiful. There was innocence to her face, but the awareness of her sexuality behind her eyes caught men off guard. Willingly, they were charmed and drawn to her. She didn't want to consider Hamil one of them.

"Cool him off before you put him in his stall. Bensen here will show you."

She hadn't seen him approach, silent as a shadow on the dusty ground. The top of his head barely reached her shoulder. He pushed aside strings of greasy hair that lay over his forehead to disclose a craggy face that looked up at her with a gaze that held an uncanny ability to diminish distance, not different than the rat hiding in the sawdust. She stepped back. For all his lack of height, the runt of a man appeared no less menacing than a sawed off shotgun.

Hamil tossed a stick to Dusty. "I see you Wednesday, Maris'. That's what he called her, having adjusted her name to roll on his tongue.

Marisa assumed the English vernacular remained a struggle for him being so foreign from his Germanic Flemish dialect. He touched the brim of his hat and went toward to barn.

It was then that she noted his curious way of going; a forward bent bobbling, as his right foot and leg turned inward, perhaps from birth or an accident. On horseback he created another dimension of art - a sweeping unison of man and beast. This man would help her achieve the same perfection. She committed herself to the goal, as she characteristically did to anything she endeavored. But Marisa knew this was different; she had been overwhelmed by a passion. Strange, she thought, watching his clumsy movements, everyone has something to conquer - their own private hurdle, real or imaginary; if you let it, that thing will destroy you; if you conquer it, you are a champion. Hers, she hadn't identified; it was an empty feeling inside her. She admired John Hamil for what he had made of himself and what he could teach her. She wondered what caused Hamil's deformity, what kind of father he was to the little blond girl, Rose-Marie, and what his life was like in that house with the woman on the veranda.

John Hamil never attended school. Hard work in the sandy ground of Flanders by the North Sea was all he could remember of his growing up years - except for the time he rode horses. First he sat on the backs of tired work animals. Then, he would trek across the dunes from his home and steal onto the property of rich aristocrats, sometimes walking for hours to find a horse at pasture to mount. He taught himself to ride without saddle or bridle, until being one with the horse was more natural that walking on his own clumsy feet. When he demonstrated his skills, he was hired as a stable boy. His meager salary paid for food and a change of ragged clothing. Every morning he walked to work and every night, after mucking out the stalls, he walked home to do tasks for his father. It wasn't long before the wealthy saw him ride and recognized his prowess. They would supplement his salary if he schooled their animals. Those high born, well-dressed ladies and gentlemen called him *Boy* but coveted his ability. Hamil found that his expertise was a needed commodity through which he could manage them. It became fashionable to boast of a horse trained by John Hamil. He set membership to the Belgian Olympic Team as his mark. If he were on the Team, he would travel and prove his superiority to the world.

At the tryouts his performance was a brilliant spectacle of talent far greater than all others. But the Olympic judges disregarded him like so much garbage, equating his birth defect as a flaw. They accepted him on the team but kept him as a backup in case injury or incident befell a primary rider. In truth, he never competed. *"Stable Boy, peasant"* they said of him, *"fit to exercise horses, groom and clean the barn but that's all."* They discredited his ability, made him look the fool. He had been used - a cold fact that stoked his energy to hate. '*Olympic Champion*', he told the world; it was a lie he had come to believe, a lie that sustained him.

Marisa Rait had aroused him. Her waist was small and she smelled warm and moist and sweet and she rubbed against him as he lifted her from the saddle. He was hard. He couldn't let her see that. He closed the door of the tack room and relieved himself of the throbbing in his groin, thinking of the other women that had affected him that way. It was not a modest list. First there was the wife of the Flemish landowner. She was the first to seduce him. She awakened his libido and he satisfied it with her daughter until they sent her away to school. Then he took what came to him. Women were all alike, rich or poor. The more abusive he was to them, the more they desired him. All he had to do was wait, they'd come with their blouses revealingly open or with an excuse to visit the barn at night. It was a bore, no conquest, but he serviced them discreetly. Like mares in heat, they wanted a stud and he availed them. It didn't take much. Mostly, they cried out. He knew he was large and they liked the pain. They spread their legs and took his brief pummeling. They used him. He found no pleasure in that, and took to doing it himself. Once in a while there was Margaret - his dutiful wife. He hoped the Rait girl would be a challenge.

***

Bensen waited while Marisa walked Scorpio on the lead until he was cool. Then he motioned for her to follow him into the barn, through the dark labyrinth of the stable. He stopped in front of an empty stall. "Here."

A heavily pregnant cat rubbed against Marisa's leg. Her back arched with affection; she was purring loudly. "Nice kitty." Marisa bent down to stroke her.

"Not so nice." Ellen Coleman, wearing a fluffy pink sweater - apparently to emphasize her femininity, emerged from the next stall. Her head was down. "She bites off their heads to eat them."

"What?" Marisa straightened up. It was a shocking remark.

"The rats. The nice kitty bites off their heads before she eats them." Ellen left the barn without another word.

Marisa had a sharp twinge of uneasiness in her stomach. It was almost enough to bring her spirits down from the fantastic high she had experienced a few minutes before. She removed the saddle, and bridle from Scorpio and fitted on his halter. Bensen was beside her, staring at her every move. His sun-beaten, heavy boned face made her uneasy. He took the tack and mutely handed her a blanket, which she put over the horse as indicated. Scorpio helped himself to a long drink of water, and greedily ate the sugar lump Marisa had had concealed in her pocket. Not wanting to leave, and having no reason to remain, she sighed, and turned to say good-bye to Bensen. He was gone. Marisa shrugged and found her way out through the side door. *"You got it,"* still echoed in her ears. Marisa smiled; she took that jump over and over again in her mind. She couldn't wait for her next lesson to recapture the sensation of that moment of thrust and flight. As she faced the barn to get into the car a glint of light caught her eye. She blinked. The sun was being reflected by a piece of metal. Squinting, she traced its source to the hayloft and saw Bensen, overhead. Watching.

CHAPTER 3

The first shot of the Civil War was fired on Fort Sumter from The Battery, downtown on Charleston Harbor. Here, now, were the homes of the *'Blue Bloods,'* built by their ancestors. They were people hard put to relinquish the culture of the Old South. The large brick structures are close together with charming courtyards abloom with flowers during most of the year. A block over from King Street, bustling with shops and restaurants, is the long, one-story building that, not so long ago, was the Slave Trade Market. Today, it housed rows of concession stands where T-shirts and antiques were sold. Sitting on the ground out front were the woman-descendants of black slaves, speaking their Gullah, a dialogue, unique to their culture and not understood by outsiders. On any afternoon in the hot summer they would be there, in the shade of the eaves, weaving their Sweet Grass baskets while mechanically swatting at the gnats that swarmed invisibly about them.

Because the marshes and islands surrounding Charleston created a natural blockade it escaped destruction during The War. Unlike any other city in the South, the pre-war buildings can be seen in their original state.

Twenty minutes north of Charleston's business-district is Sullivan's Island, where the young, well-to-do up-starts were building custom homes. After their marriage, Warren offered to build Marisa whatever house she wished there on the beach, but she preferred Mt. Pleasant and a house with history. Better, she thought, to become part of the stew-pot than to parent complaining timber not yet pliant to running feet, walls that have heard no secrets, nor windows that have seen no humanity. She renovated a landmark house built on pylons giving a wonderful visage of the expansive Cooper River Bridge. It gave her pleasure to look across the harbor to Sullivan Island and The Battery where her parents still lived surrounded by polished mahogany, glittering crystal, silk and velvet. She never felt at home in that house, it was merely the address where she lived during her growing up years. Home meant love, sharing and laughter, what she dreamed she would create for her own family.

Marisa parked her car in the garage, which had served as a carriage-house in yesteryears, and walked up the flight of stairs to the living quarters. A Willow Tree shaded the verandah; there was always a pleasant breeze. She loved her house and everything in it. Warren and she had spent a happy year combing antique shops, searching for each piece. Especially, she liked the bathroom where he installed a Jacuzzi for her in the claw-footed tub. Marisa hooked the heel of her boot into the bootjack and pulled out her foot, removed her breeches and was soon submerged in a warm bath, glad that she had asked Warren to bring something home for dinner. Cooking was out of the question today.

By the time the aches and pains of strained muscles eased the first draft of her article on John Hamil and The Hunt was formulated in her mind. She slipped on a red caftan and sat down at her computer. She was still working when Warren came in with a bag of Chinese food and his partner, Chez D'Acarti. The two men were a team: Warren, with his square jaw, and a sense of humor behind soft brown eyes that challenged his would-be arrogance; and Chez, his love of life and cultivated Latin good looks were disarming - both strong bodied and suntanned, their dark hair streaked with light from long days working outside on the construction sites. Marisa was always glad to see Chez.

For as long as Warren could remember he dreamed of being a builder. His father's plumbing business ultimately expanded to real-estate, but dealt only with transactions at the candy store level. Warren's head was filled with the hope of building for people to expand the dreams of their life.

Soon after he left college Warren had started his own construction business, doing all the negotiating, banking and contracting work himself, plus the blueprints for the development of *Raittown*. He wasn't a religious man, nor was he superstitious but he believed it was an intervention from above that caused the cement truck to stop at the building site that day, six years ago. Out jumped the oddest looking of cement men. He was of average height, clean-shaven, wearing khaki pants and a fresh white shirt. A spreading toothy smile became his prominent feature. Heavy work gloves were tucked into his belt.

"You need work done, eh? I got time and I do the best job." He spoke quickly and confidently with a heavy Italian accent.

Warren had much work that needed to be done, but his budget was too thin to lay out cash payments in advance that the large firms demanded.

"This truck here is mine. There's nothing with cement, and stone I don't do. My name is Caesare D'Acarti - Chez, Mr. Rait." He stuck out his hand.

Warren liked his gumption. "How did you know my name?"

"I do my homework. Hop in. I'll show you some of my work."

"Just a minute. Who do you work with? Where are you from?"

"Me?" He laughed, "I'm from this truck," and patted his vehicle. "We work alone. Wherever this truck is, that's where I'm from."

"You accept thirty days' payment for your jobs?"

"Chez grinned. "Yeah, as long as I got work the money will come in."

Warren nodded. "Let's take a ride."

Chez stopped, and pointed out completed building foundations bordered by vast parking lots enhanced by raised islands for planting in the soon to be completed shopping mall.

Warren was impressed. "You've done all that?"

"Life's more than a can of beer and a television set. You gotta make the right connections. Jobs. Money doesn't come to the hardest worker, it's who you know. I heard of you, Mr. Rait. You like to get your hands dirty, and you need a partner."

"Stop here," Warren said. They had been driving northward, up the peninsula into the neck area. "See that stretch of meadow and the woods behind it. Those fifteen acres are mine. I need foundations put down, along with curbs, dry wells, and septic tanks. Finish the job in three months, and you've found yourself a partner."

"That's fourteen houses." Chez examined the blueprints that Warren unrolled, and spread over the fender of the truck. He rubbed his chin. "You've got a deal."

It turned out that Caesare D'Acarti was a Michelangelo of cement; he hired a crew and brought the job in on time. Warren drew up the partnership contracts. Soon they became the trendsetters of affordable housing. At the end of two years there were four *Raittown* sites under construction.

During dinner the two men joked about the day and brainstormed about tomorrow. Soon Marisa tired of listening, excused herself and went to bed feeling like she had nothing to add. It wasn't always like that.

She and Warren started dating after they had met at her father's party. She was in her freshman year at The College of Charleston; studying journalism. He was taking a graduate engineering course at Citadel. He was strong minded, and gentle, and listened to her ideas and dreams, and shared his with her. They laughed together, and were not afraid to cry together. He filled her life with the love she so missed as a child. Physically it was magnetism. Marisa was a contemporary woman. When she married Warren she was not clinically a virgin, but emotionally she was. Her wedding gown was fit for a princess and the lavish reception at the Yacht Club became the event of the year. Marisa cared for none of it. She had left all preparations in the capable hands of her mother. Frances Lawner was a domineering gregarious woman, who sought approval in the social spotlight; she rose gallantly to the occasion. To Marisa all that mattered, all that she remembered, was walking down the aisle of the church to her groom, and the love she saw in Warren's eyes; their fingers intertwined as they took their vows to be united forever in holy matrimony.

Warren was already established in business. Marisa, being of like character left school and found a job for a weekly community news publication covering school events, and church celebrations. It was not satisfactory. This relating of births, weddings and deaths was not for a serious news reporter; it was more the job of a census taker. She sent article after article to the editor at the Charleston Post. Either he recognized her talent or was worn down by her perseverance; Rob MacGrath finally put her on staff.

She and Warren each became absorbed in their own careers. Without notice the urgency of their passion dwindled, and their time together lost priority. The first morning she awoke to find Warren already gone to work she let her mind go back to the early time of their marriage when his lips - the closeness of him was the breath of her existence. She clung to that time and grieved its passing.

***

As usual, Warren was already at work when she got up the next morning. She dressed quickly, grabbed her portfolio, and rushed out to the newspaper office, too anxious to show the editor her article than to let disappointment spoil her day.

Rob MacGrath was a large Scotsman who spoke quietly and rolled his 'R's like his parental clan. It delighted Marisa. "Mac, you trill like a canary." She teased when they sat on the balcony drinking coffee while he did the final edit of her article. Introverted about his personal life with a fiery constitution, he expressed himself through the written word. He feared no one, printed nothing but the truth, the whole truth without being accused of

running a tabloid. He used to be a professional line-
-backer, using bulk not words for recognition - until
an injury to his knees put an end to football. He
wasn't saddened. *"How else would I have
discovered that who I am is a newspaperman?"* He
would say. Two years after becoming editor-in-
chief of the Charleston Post its daily circulation
doubled. When Marisa Rait came along he
connected with her aggressive resourcefulness, and
gave her a weekly column, telling her to choose a
pen-name for the controversial articles for which, he
thought. she was suited. Anonymity would give her
freedom. Readers trusted they were being informed
of the unbiased truth. Her column made *regular
people* important. No one knew the true identity of
Leslie Allen.

'*Grand Central Station*' is what MacGrath's
much trafficked office was affectionately called.
One after another, people filed in and out of the
editor's office. To avoid the constant interrupting
knock, he replaced the wooden door with a glass
one so people could see that he was busy, and wait
for his signal to enter. Upon arrival, Marisa saw he
was with a gentleman, and was surprised when
MacGrath waved her in. Their business apparently
over, the young man picked up his sports jacket,
and was walking past her when he hesitated, looked
at her face, and smiled.

"Marisa Rait this is Brad Novick, he's a
music producer. Brad took a full page ad every day
and Sunday for two weeks." It was a casual
introduction.

She nodded, thinking he was going to say something but he continued out of the office. She closed the door behind him. "Mac, I saw The Hunt." She handed him the outline for her article. "And I was at the farm, even took a lesson. Mac, I'm a good rider, and didn't know it. He wants me in a class, and I'll take private lessons. He also said something about joining The Hunt, but that's pushing it. Anyway, I'll have plenty of opportunity to listen and poke around."

Y're to substantiate the rumors about Hamil Farm not put y'rself in jeopardy. Y're fine t'me, Marisa, y'know that well. There have been too many casualties, and talk of injured horses out there. No one's ever made a legal accusation. That's the mystery. No one's ever complained. No one's said anything."

"All the people I've seen around the barn, including his daughter, and probably his wife, are obsessed by him. It's wicked the way he verbally punishes his students. I don't know what he must do to the horses."

MacGrath took a soft leather bound book from beneath the piles of paper on his desk. "Some solicitor sent this." He riffled the blank pages. "Use it for a journal, but keep it well hidden. Remember it's the work of *Leslie Allen*. No one can link you to the paper, no one."

"No one knows, Mac. I haven't even told Warren about the article. You don't mind if I tell him, do you?"

"No, but that's where it ends. Make sure he understands that. And Marisa, we'll do the story in

44

installments. First we'll print the facts as you know them, arouse suspicion and anger, and the demand for an answer to the big question – '*WHY?* Then we'll expose him. It won't be easy to find out."

"Many readers have children who take lessons at Hamil Farm, it's our responsibility to alert them." She closed the journal inside her portfolio wondering what those pages would reveal once filled.

Mac shook his head. "Why would anyone take that abuse? It's only horseback riding, for heaven's sake."

"No Mac, it's more. Riding and hunting are part of the culture in Charleston and John Hamil is an icon."

"A way of life, yes, but this is more than bumps and bruises. Last year there were two tragedies. A young girl, ten years old, fell off and died in the hospital; a kid that age doesn't have experience to be jumping an Olympic Course. Another guy had a spinal-cord injury; he's still in re-hab. There are many stables for lessons and boarding with a clean slate. Why Hamil? Don't underestimate him, Marisa. He's cunning"

The telephone on his desk was ringing. The secretary was buzzing the intercom.

"I don't know what his charm or power is, but when people, and horses are injured, and no one files a complaint there's a reason." Mac pressed.

The intercom persisted.

Mac answered. "Hold my calls." He said impatiently. He turned back to Marisa. "Keep your eyes and ears open. Sure he'll try to find out who's writing the articles."

"I'm careful." She stretched up on tiptoes to kiss his cheek and opened the door. It nearly hit Brad Novick in the face. "Oh, sorry, I didn't see you."

"Excuse me. I think I left my address book on the desk. May I go in to look?'

The editor stepped aside. "Go on in. It's probably there under the ad layouts." He turned back to Marisa. "It could be dangerous. Y' can say no."

"Are you kidding? I'm taking a lesson tomorrow."

"Here it is." Brad said from behind them. He patted the big man on the shoulder and left.

"Marisa, y'can say no." The editor's eyes showed more than professional concern.

Marisa waved to him as she went out the door. MacGrath went into his office. It wasn't a moment before he was busy with his next appointment.

CHAPTER 4

Brad Novick was waiting for her when she came outside. "You have printers ink on your cheek."

She looked up into amused gray eyes.

"May I...?" He took a handkerchief from his jacket pocket, gently tipped up her chin, and wiped a streak from her face. Her mouth was just below his.

She blushed.

"Do you work for the paper?"

"No, I'm a friend of Rob MacGrath." She lied.

"What did he mean when he told you to keep your eyes and ears open, that it was dangerous?"

Marisa coughed, and fumbled in her handbag for a tissue, using the time to fabricate her story. "I collect Civil War memorabilia, so does he, not uniforms or weapons but letters, documents, and engraved jewelry. It's fascinating."

"That doesn't sound perilous."

"Where there's money there's greed. He was warning me not to spend a lot of time verifying the provenance of a piece and draw attention; a dealer could snatch it up from under my nose."

"And I thought antique collecting was for idle matrons."

"Right, and I thought R and B is just for teeny-boppers."

Brad laughed. "Speaking of noses, I missed a spot right here on the tip."

She stepped back, aware that she had let a perfect stranger touch her face. "You are rude and presumptuous." She got in her car and drove away from Brad Novick.

The next morning Marisa awoke early to find Warren had already left the house. Clearly, the construction of Raittown was assuming the characteristics of a monument - to himself, she thought indignantly. Sunlight was streaming through the bedroom window, making a checkerboard pattern on the white walls. She stretched languidly and thought of Brad Novick, how his touch had stirred her. *"Silly,"* but she couldn't deny it.

By the time Marisa arrived at Hamil Farm she was in a snit. Warren had left in the morning without a word. She hadn't had a chance to tell him of her assignment, not even about her lessons. She wouldn't have mentioned the potential danger as Mac had called it. Surely, that was an exaggeration of what was merely the odd behavior of a stringent teacher with an unpredictable soft side. *'Accidents happen'*. Still, she would like to have told her husband where she was going. Also the large festering wound she saw on Scorpio's belly didn't do anything to make her spirits soar. At once she sought to question John Hamil.

She went out of the barn. The angel-haired child was cantering toward her on a brown pony. Maria waved. The girl reined up beside her.

"I'm Marisa. I have a lesson with your father. What's your name?"

"Rose-Marie." Long bangs fell over her forehead.

"I saw you going to school the other morning. I wore a uniform just like yours. No classes for you today, Rose-Marie?"

"Yes ma'am, but Father said I have to stay here and practice on Cinnamon for the Brookvale Horse Show next week. He wants a blue ribbon for the Hamil Farm entry in every class. He's working in the paddock now with her, but you can never bother him when he's working with the horses."

Marisa handed a lollypop up to Rose-Marie. She brought it hoping she would get a chance to speak to the child. "Don't worry, your father won't know I'm here until it's time for my lesson. I want to ask him about this wound on Scorpio. Did you see…?"

Without taking the candy, Rose-Marie spurred her horse, and galloped back toward the house.

Marisa looked after her. Mac had told her the gossip about John Hamil and his jewel – the daughter he was polishing in his image. It was said he trained her rigorously and some were concerned for her safety. Just last year, at the Jump Off competition for The Junior American Equestrian Team, Rose-Marie was riding Atta Boy, the famed and beloved horse that had brought her father so many championships in America. Atta Boy shied, refused a fence. Rose-Marie was thrust headlong into the rail. A splinter gashed her head, barely missing her right eye. For Hamil the scar became a constant reminder of his daughter's disgrace – of *his* disgrace. Rose-Marie tried to keep it out of sight beneath her hair. Later there were whispers about Atta Boy's mysterious disappearance. But, what no one knew was that it was her father with whom Rose-Marie climbed into bed during a thunder storm, and he who rocked her in his arms during a feverish siege of Measles.

Marisa led Scorpio onto the field as Ellen Coleman, on her horse, London Fog, was leaving. Ellen wasn't talkative but she was a face to greet, and since their horses were in neighboring stalls Marisa thought they might groom them together, talk and become friends. She waved to Ellen, and saw John Hamil on the outside course. He was mounted on Cinnamon, the filly he was training for Rose-Marie.

"Good-morning, Mr. Hamil." She called. "Could you look at this bruise on Scorpio? Do you know what happened to him?"

"He caught himself on something in the stall, Maris'."

"But, Mr. Hamil, I checked, there is nothing in the stall that could have hurt him." She insisted.

He regarded her moment. When at last he spoke, the words were short and clipped. "He be fine. We practice on the flat here, then we do the low jumps. You enter the horse show here the first week in March."

Maria's heart skipped a beat. She took a deep breath, and was filled with elation. Hamil said she would be competitive to show. She checked her girth, making sure it didn't rub Scorpio's injury, and mounted. At the end of the lesson, she arranged with Hamil that she would rent Scorpio, in that way she would be the only one to ride him. 'It could have been that another rider had made the girth too tight, or kicked him with a sharp spur.'

After cooling off her horse, brushing him and mucking out the stall, she was ready to leave. She stopped the car at the end of the driveway, her head spinning with Hamil's compliment: she would be in the horse show, he would be her sponsor. Marisa took out her hidden journal and was about to write when she saw Brad Novick leaning beside his BMW. She quickly put the journal inside her portfolio, and lowered the window. "Whatever are you doing here?" She wasn't sure if she were annoyed or pleased to see him.

"I heard you telling MacGrath that you'd be here for a lesson. I thought I'd stop and see you again. You must be hungry. How about lunch? There's a lovely inn down the road."

She didn't realize, yes, she was hungry. She followed him in her car to the aptly named Willows on the Pond Inn. He sat beside her in the booth, in the dusky curtained dining room. They ordered hamburgers. She had lemonade, he a beer. Talk came easily. She was glad he was there to listen, glad to be able to let out her feelings and not have to keep them all bottled up inside. She told him of the majesty of The Hunt and the sense of power she felt going over her first jump. Oh, if Warren had been the one to talk to, she wouldn't be sitting next to a man she had just met, pouring out her heart, and leading him on to think there could be more between them than lemonade and beer. Warren would be all she needed.

And it seemed to Brad that riding in The Hunt meant as much to Marisa as innovative music did to him. Perhaps, too, it filled a similar emptiness. He asked her about her life, about her marriage, and why she was riding now with Hamil. These questions were hard for her to answer truthfully, not wanting to disclose her empty life with her husband or that she was writing for the newspaper. All that had become secondary. '*Why was she there*?' She knew she wasn't the same woman who had first walked up that hill to watch The Hunt, and she knew she wasn't being *Leslie Allen* writing another thriller story for MacGrath. Something was in her blood, a passion that started when she went over her first hurdle, and John Hamil said: "You got it."

"I was married." Brad said soberly. "My wife's name was Angela. She was all the name implies to a Roman Catholic - devout and virginal. Two weeks after the wedding she allowed me to consummate the marriage. A month later she was pregnant. After that I had to sleep on the damask sofa that her parents had given us along with the house. She refused to leave the bedroom. The house was filthy; there was no cooking. In her fourth month she had a miscarriage. She said I caused her stress, which *"twisted her insides."* The doctor said if she conceived again, it could kill her. From then on she lived in repentance for the sin she had committed by leaving the church, and marrying me. Before the year was over I left her - her and her family's fortune. Now, at thirty-four years old, I have a business I enjoy and respect for myself."

"You're a record promoter. What exactly do you do?"

"I work for the recording companies, and directly with the program directors of the radio stations to add a song to their playlist. There are twenty-eight stations that play music in the tri-county region of Charleston, and I travel to all of them. I'm good at what I do. If music isn't heard it won't sell." He smiled at her, pushed back the table, stood and offered his arm to help her up. "Let's take a walk; the bartender here mixes a beautiful negroni - the color of a rose. Come, before you go, I'd like to give you a rose outside beneath the tree."

They walked along the stream that emptied into the pond, and stopped to sip the negroni in the shade of the Willow Trees that dipped down to touch the water.

"Did you love your wife when you married her?"

"At thirty-one I was still travelling around chasing after rock bands, smoking marijuana - the whole scene. She was all I wasn't. I thought we could make a successful marriage. No, I didn't love Angela."

Marisa threw a stone into the water and watched the broadening ripples. He took her hand as they walked silently among the trees, each lost in their own thoughts but connected by the warmth of their fingers.

It became a routine she valued: her lesson at Hamil Farm then lunch with Brad at the inn or beneath the trees from a basket that he brought from the restaurant. She started the relationship on the pretext of a friendship, denying it was to find open arms and a resting place, to find what she had lost with Warren. Marisa had never had an affair, never imagined she would, but she knew if she continued to see Brad Novick it would happen. Being honest with herself, she was anxious for it to happen. It would be something that had no more to do with her love for Warren than her preparations to be in a horse show. She was taking nothing from Warren. He had no time for her and physically he was cold. Lately, when they did make love, it was only their bodies that touched. There were no words of sentiment, no playful teasing or laughter, no physical learning as when they were first married. He had been closed to her for so long that now it was impossible to let the touch of his hand awaken any desire. 'What if he were having an affair?' She had to wonder, "What secrets did Warren have? Everyone has a secret'. In her mind, to spiritually desert your mate for business and money for your own self-esteem was a greater 'cheat' than a loveless intimacy between two people.

Warren Rait sat at the wheel of his Jaguar wondering why the seat didn't feel comfortable of late. Looking back, he realized that building another "*Raittown*" was really pampering himself. The costs were exorbitant. Every phase of the project needed an infusion of cash and he had exhausted the banks. The work hours were ruinous. Warren hadn't told Marisa of their desperate financial position that threatened to change their life style, certainly to change the way he thought about himself. He couldn't bear to have her see him as a failure. Though he pretended not to notice, it was apparent that the relationship with his wife had changed. 'We used to complete each other. Now we are just two people living under the same roof.' Warren reflected. Whereas before he had been the boy wonder with everyone clamoring to back him, now he was avoided, wasting precious hours accomplishing nothing. No wonder he couldn't sleep at night; no wonder he was impossible to speak to. His mind was in too many places; his thoughts getting too tangled into fears, his view of the future empty with only himself to blame.

Today's meeting with Chez would focus on all he had shut his mind to over the last six months. They were going bankrupt. Busto! People weren't buying houses. You just couldn't get a mortgage. He waited for the challenge to fire his blood; it only added to his frustration, and he fell into a depression to which he felt entitled. A man creates a life-style for himself and his family, and gets comfortable in the groove. Stepping out of it - stepping down might destroy him. Warren's self-image was his strength.

***

Christmas passed and Marisa spent four days a week riding at Hamil Farm: twice for lessons and two times to exercise Scorpio, after each she met Brad at the inn, always anxious to tell him of her triumphs. Many times she ducked into the storage barn to change into a dress, wanting to please Brad. 'A man likes to see a lady looking feminine - not always in boots'.

Brad had rented a room at the inn. It was centrally located in his work region. When Marisa arrived he helped her out of the car, took her arm, and propelled her inside.

"What's the hurry?"

"In five minutes the radio station is playing my new song. I have to hear it. I'm glad you came in time to give me a commentary. Come." He was walking up the stairs. She hesitated.

"Don't worry, I won't seduce you unless you ask me." He laughed.

"Monster." She cried, and chased him upstairs.

The music was playing. He stood with her, took her in his arms, and rocked gently to the rhythm. It was strange being in another man's arms, though she had imagined it. It was thrilling to feel her body come alive, and responsive after sleeping in a cold bed with Warren for six months.

"Do you like it?" Brad whispered.

"Heaven." She said raising her hand to the back of his neck with no thought of the song.

He kissed her lips softly.

She answered his kiss with awakened desire.

Their lovemaking was unrestrained and uninhibited. Marisa was surprised that she was capable of such erotic freedom with a man that was not her husband. When it was over she slept in his arms, contented and delighted with herself. After a while he led her to the shower and tossed her a cake of pine scented soap. "Go to work," he said, stepping inside,

"She nudged him under the steaming water. "Oh, you are beautiful," She laughed, lathering his long hair and forming it into a peak.

They washed one another slowly, moving their hands over their lover's body to memorize the curves.

She didn't see him get to his knees. She tried to move away but his mouth was hotter than the water falling on her back and she gave way to spasms of exquisite rapture. She was dizzy and thought she would fall, but then he straightened up and carried her to the bed. In one fluid motion he lowered himself into her. She was so utterly possessed by her own pleasure that she didn't feel him tremor inside her. The final wave came when his fingers gripped her shoulders. His whole body stiffened for a moment and he gasped.

They lay like that for a few minutes. Marisa didn't want to move or open her eyes.

"Would you believe next time it will be even better?" He whispered almost inaudibly, his lips brushing her ear.

"I don't believe it."

"This time you shower alone."

Afterward, she dried herself quickly and dressed to leave.

"Be careful, now that you are mine, Marisa. I don't like you jumping those horses."

***

The Charleston Post published an article by *Leslie Allen* about Hamil Farm in the paper's Sunday edition. It did not cause the stir that the editor, Rob MacGrath, and Marisa had hoped. There wasn't much to report, only that boarders and students were unnaturally reserved and that no one spoke to each other. They moved about with blinders, even when they found injuries on their horses – expensive horses. *"Why was Hamil able to demean so many well-respected people with a glance or verbal attack?* The reporter arose many questions, but could not supply any satisfactory answers. As for Hamil as an instructor? He was deserving of praise. All of his students excelled in equitation regardless of painful falls, and some broken bones. The article imparted little gossip but the seed of an inquisition was planted.

He didn't know who he was looking for; *Leslie Allen* could be a man or a woman. It was a unisex name he was told, though it made no sense to him. He'd done some investigating and found that the columnist, the person who wrote the article, might not be the one doing the snooping. No matter, if questioned he had a simple answer. It was posted inside the tack room and above the door as you entered the indoor riding space. *"Ride at your own risk."* Legally that disclaimer cleared him. Not even a hungry, ambulance-chasing lawyer would waste time on such a claim.

Hamil slept well that night.

CHAPTER 5

New Years day was a week away when Marisa
came to the stall to find another injury on Scorpio's
belly. Hamil was astride a large Bay outside the
barn. When she showed him the wound he merely
tipped his hat. "We do the lesson on the field." He
trotted off down the slope. Marisa mounted
Scorpio; she met him by the first obstacle.

"Start with The Coop, Maris'. Watch your
approach."

She was about to inquire again about
Scorpio but clearly the lesson had begun.

Marisa obediently turned Scorpio's head to
face the redwood, inverted wedge. She
concentrated on correct form. Successful execution
of a jump depends on the rider's perspective,
balance and weight distribution, an uninterrupted
thrust of the animal's powerful hind legs and
freedom of his neck to pull him forward. She
estimated the distance from the obstacle and gave
Scorpio the signal to jump. The horse rose from the
ground.

"Maris'!" Hamil called to her sharply.
Instinctively, she turned her head and then,
attempting to regain her spot of concentration, lost

her balance. In an effort to keep her seat, she grabbed Scorpio's mane. The reins dropped from her hands. Scorpio's hooves barely missed getting tangled in the length of slack leather. When the horse stopped, she slid from the saddle. Uninjured, she lay a moment to catch her breath. Scorpio was grazing next to her. Hamil looked down from his horse with no inclination to help.

"Maris', you were behind the action. Remount. Stay close."

Dumbly, she obeyed and managed to get back in the saddle.

Hamil trotted over the fence, and out of the field, crossed the road, and went into the woods, galloping along the narrow path with Scorpio following. Marisa had to duck to avoid the sharp branches that reached out to scratch her face. A sapling lashed her cheek. Faster and faster, they galloped along the path. Hamil jumped fallen trees, a rocky stream. Pull as she may, there was no way to slow or stop her speeding horse. They made a sharp turn to the left toward Hamil Farm, and ran up a hill. On the crest loomed an overgrown stone wall. Marisa closed her eyes, realizing that she was not at all in control. The distance closed and she was over the wall flying detached from the rest of the world. It was Scorpio who took her safely over the barrier. He trotted to a halt. Marisa pushed her hunt cap back into position. John Hamil was riding toward her.

"I fill out the entry form for you. You be in the horse show in March. This fall you be in The

Hunt." He reined about abruptly and cantered to the barn.

Marisa took a minute to realize what had occurred. She had qualified. Already, she could smell the pungency of sweat mingled with fresh blood when the gore of the dead fox would be smeared across her face in the traditional ceremony of one's Maiden Hunt. Soon it would be time for her initiation. She knew full well that the picture of her own face as a bloody mask should revolt her. It didn't.

"He must think you're doing well if he took you out on the trail alone." Ellen said in a half-hearted voice when Marisa led Scorpio into the barn, her face flushed and shining. Ellen had been riding at Hamil Farm for three years and disliked the prospect of another rider capturing the teacher's attention but she thought Marisa was ignorant of those jealousies and she did deserve to be complimented.

"Thanks, I feel as if it's the greatest thing I've ever done. Did you feel the same when you started?"

"Everyone does with Hamil. If you don't, you're out." She was rubbing the side of her leg with her palm, seemingly a nervous habit Marisa had seen her do whenever speaking of the instructor. 'He takes over your mind. He dictates your thinking; you have no choices. Once you've come this far it's no longer a sport. It's madness."

In appearance Ellen was on the refreshing side of plain - her brown hair slicked back in a knot. With a little styling and make-up, Marisa thought, she would be a smart looking woman. If she moved with more self-confidence her lanky athletic body would have been the envy of every woman who sweated in daily workout classes at the gym. No doubt her stretch breeches and tall brown hunt boots emphasized her attributes.

"Did you join The Hunt with him?" Marisa asked.

Ellen turned and busied herself adjusting her horse's halter. Never would she forget that crisp morning of the season's opening foxhunt? "I was a novice then." Ellen reflected. "Though I'd been riding only eight months, I felt I was ready. Fog was well schooled and obedient. I was ready. Actually, I'd been ready to hunt for as far back as I can remember. My parents never allowed me to ride. I used to daydream about joining a foxhunt when other girls worried about being asked for a Saturday night date. I started to ride after I was married. Larry, my husband, finally consented when both kids were of school age."

"And Hamil was your teacher?"

"Yes." She lifted her head. "He gave me a lot of attention. I thought he singled me out because I showed promise. I worked. Christ, how I worked. When he invited me to join The Hunt...". Her words trailed off; she was suddenly preoccupied, distant, looking beyond the field into the woods.

Marisa interrupted and brought her back. "Ellen, did he watch to see if you could keep the pace with so much company?"

Ellen faced her squarely. "That's just it." Her lips quivered as she spoke. "He didn't even stop when I fell going over the stream. No one stopped. They all followed him, and kept going, leaving me alone in the woods, crying in such pain that I couldn't move. It was an hour before the ambulance arrived. Do you think he came to the hospital? No, I couldn't believe it. I was laid up with a shattered tibia, immobile for nearly one month, and then I lugged that heavy cast around with crutches for three more months. Still, not a phone call. Nothing. And he never left my mind, Marisa. I really thought he cared for me. Then I felt guilty; I had let him down. I was the disappointment. Despite the pain and disillusionment, I'm here at Hamil Farm, and if he invites me to hunt, I'll be out there again on Sunday morning." She looked at Marisa quizzically. "I don't understand myself."

For the first time Ellen was speaking to her as a friend, but she had no explanation, and so she met her gaze and remained silent. Obviously, Ellen would do as told with no regard to her well=being.; thus she had thrown away her life insurance. This dependence was suicidal. 'Why did she let the man govern her mind and body?' It was all the more frightening to Marisa because in the weeks she had been at Hamil Farm she sensed that she too, in a bizarre manner, had given up some of her own self-control.

Scorpio probed her pocket for a hidden carrot.

"Ellen, do you know what happened to Scorpio? He didn't get this gash in the stall, as Mr. Hamil would like me to believe. There's nothing in there to hurt him. I checked for nails and changed the bedding. It's something he doesn't want me to know."

Ellen averted her eyes. It was a habit that maddened Marisa for it meant the subject was closed.

"Please, Ellen, if you know anything tell me. I feel responsible."

"It can only be what Mr. Hamil says."
It seemed to Marisa that the subject of John Hamil did not bear discussion with Ellen or anyone else at Hamil Farm.

"What happened to you?" Ellen asked, only now seeing Marisa's grass-stained breeches,

"Nothing, on the same basis that nothing happened to Scorpio. I'm going to ask Hamil to have a vet check this wound." She hooked the gate of the stall and turned to leave.

Ellen grabbed her arm. "Marisa, ...don't. Don't ask Hamil. It's his barn and his horse. He always vets his horses himself. Don't ask him, Marisa."

They looked at each other for a prolonged moment, and Marisa could see fear in Ellen's eyes. She wondered if her own ride behind Hamil had been a test of ability or a lesson in discipline. Perhaps he had caused her to fall. Had she no right to ask him about Scorpio's injury? There was more to the unexplained wound than what he was telling her, and she suspected that Ellen knew more than she would speak about. "I'll see you here on Friday." She said preparing to leave.

"Marisa, you don't understand," stammered the girl.

"Yes, Ellen, I understand. John Hamil has a strange magnetism, yet everyone is afraid of him. What I don't understand is 'why?' He's a good instructor, and has a good barn. Nothing alarming."

At that moment, Ellen's face drained of color. Marisa whirled around to see Bensen leaning against the wall. In his hand was a heavy pitchfork.

"Bensen." Marisa started forward. "Do you know what happened to Scorpio? Did you see this injury?" She stroked the horse's flank. Those were the first words she had spoken to the man since they met. In the past she had avoided him whenever possible. He looked capable of the most sinister trick, yet she had never heard him utter a word or do anything that prompted her foreboding. Under ordinary circumstances she would have attributed it to her over-zealous imagination, but nothing at Hamil Farm was ordinary.

He jabbed the formidable fork into a bale of hay, and heaved it into Scorpio's stall muttering under his breath. As he approached, the horse shied away, slamming his body against the wall, wild eyed. The quick spinning movement caused a cloud of sawdust to rise in the small space. Bensen pushed strands of stringy black hair from his face and wiped his eyes. It was an innocent gesture but as he did so Marisa saw Bensen with the intense clarity of a nightmare. His eyes were as black, and as malevolent as those of the barn rat hiding in his hole. Those eyes revealed to Marisa what Ellen had been warning her about. *Bensen played dumb, but reported everything he saw, and heard to John Hamil.* Thus, nothing at Hamil Farm was the result of happenstance which is why, she concluded, Scorpio's injury was none of her business.

Marisa left the barn, dug her car key from her pocket and unlocked the car. She tossed her saddle in the rear, and took her canvas bag of fresh clothing into the storage barn across from the main building. The sun beamed in from the small high windows, leaving most of the musty quarters in darkness. She made her way around the various components of white fence obstacles, a wheel-barrel, a tall box painted as a brick wall topped with a dried hedge. There were two horses there, but one stall was empty except for low stacks of baled hay. From her bag, she took her brown suede trousers, a sweater of the same cocoa shade and a pair of white lacey bikini panties, which she laid on top of the bale. The air was cold; she began to undress quickly. adept at her transformation as Clark Kent was to Superman, and would soon emerge the fashionably dressed lady one would expect to meet on Broad Street. She pulled off her boots and socks, sprinkled baby powder on her feet, and stepped into a pair of stacked-heel sandals. Usually, at this time she thought of Brad - where they would go, the games they would play. But today the mysteries of this place crowded her mind. 'If Bensen was a sentinel for John Hamil, what secret was he guarding?' John Hamil had forcibly issued a warning to her. He purposely distracted her while going over the jump by calling her name, causing her to lose her balance and fall. Surely, it had been, as she thought - a lesson to stop her interfering; he was not to be questioned.

She unhooked her bra, stepped out of the cotton briefs, put them in her bag, dusted her body with powder and stepped into the scant bikini.

John Hamil was a cruel disciplinarian. Nevertheless, only he could help her achieve the ability to ride in the hunt, and win blue ribbons in the show circuit. Truth was she needed John Hamil. Once he began teaching her, feeding her ego with his recognition, she couldn't leave. Hamil controlled her through her own ambition. It was the same with Ellen.

Marisa heard a faint mewing; looking around she saw nothing. Following the sound to a dark corner behind a bale of hay, she discovered the gray mother cat licking, and nursing her new litter. The door to the barn creaked open. Marisa shivered, and turned to find her sweater. Instead, she saw Hamil. The dog, Dusty trotted beside him. Embarrassed, she crossed her arms over her bare chest, and stepped back into the shadows. "Mr. Hamil, I was just changing my clothes to go to the city. I..."

He laid his gloved hand on her arm, and drew her into the spot of light. The brim of his hat was down.

"Please, I'm cold." She groped for her sweater.

"Stand still." He ordered, and she froze in fear at the menacing tone.

He walked around her, inspecting her - examining her ankles, her thighs, as he would a horse. She felt the rough glove run down her spine, over her buttocks scratching her skin. She dared not move. He raised his hands to her ribs, now to her shoulders and turned her around. Slowly, he removed one glove, then the other glove.

These were not the calloused stubby hands of a farm worker. The fingers were long and lean; they were smooth and white.

"A man can be judged be his hands." He held them out for her to admire. "Mine are of an aristocrat. I always work with my gloves on." He slipped his fingers inside the elastic of her panties.

"No, please, no."

He showed no concern to her frantic calls...no one was coming. The ghostly hands moved over her body pinching, probing.

"You could be an excellent rider, Maris'. I will ride with you in many shows. I will carry you with me into a world that will pay homage to your talent. I can make you a renowned rider. You'd like that, wouldn't you?"

She was only aware of his fingers worming through her pubic hair.

"Wouldn't you?" He said emphatically.

She recoiled but nodded obediently.

"But you must learn never to say 'no', and never to ask anything. I don't tolerate questions, Maris'." He looked into her eyes, and removed his hand.

She clenched her teeth, unable to cry out. The message had been unmistakable. She was forced to stand there in submission.

Hamil took her right hand in his and pushed it under her breast. "Show me, Maris'. Hold it out to me. Are you beautiful? Are you worthy of my beautiful hands? Are you worthy of my time?"

She shuddered, crying soundlessly

He traced his forefinger slowly from her neck to her nipple. It was hard. "See how anxious you are. You were more subtle than other women in the class, but your signal was clear. You waited for me to lift you from the saddle. You wanted to feel me."

"No." She ashamedly remembered wondering what kind of lover he was. Had it shown in her eyes? But she hadn't wanted him. She hadn't. It's a thought she had of every man she saw who was above others in one way or another: athletes, politicians, men of science or the arts; it was a natural curiosity that most women have. Women are no different than men in their thoughts. It wasn't unnatural. It wasn't lust. She tried to break away.

He pulled her kicking and twisting body close to him, slapped her face and clamped his hand across her mouth. "Stand as you were. Show me your body. Offer it to me. Perhaps I will have you."

Her trembling lips were parted and her breasts were rising and falling with erratic breathing she couldn't control. His touch pricked her flesh.

He rubbed each breast she pushed out to him with his palm, and then smiled as he squeezed her nipples, one at a time with those foul inhuman fingers. All the while he stared intently into her face, enjoying her distress.

Her breath was coming in gasps. She tried to look away from his eyes.

"Take off your pants."

She didn't move.

He stood a moment, waiting, his eyes mocking her.

She remained immobile.

He bent down, and picked up his glove to put it on. "I don't think you'd like me to do it for you." He grinned.

Marisa removed the tiny garment. She was naked. His lips formed a satisfied smile. He dropped the glove.

The white hands moved over her hips, down the outside of each leg to her feet and up to the inside of her thighs. His fingers explored the moist folds of her body.

"No! Oh, no!" She cried at the indignity and forced her leaden arms against his shoulders to shove him away.

He threw her forward over the bale of hay, moved his hands over her buttocks and the area, most sensitive, beneath. He encircled her with his arms from the rear; his fingers teased and toyed with her nipples.

Tears stung the welts on her cheeks where he'd slapped her. She tried to stand but his weight pressed on her back.

"Stop it…get off me. Damn you! Damn you!"

"Shh, Maris'. Shh, no one will come. You are in my barn of your own accord. Hush now." He shoved his knee between her legs, working it up and down. "You are ready, Maris'." He unzipped his pants and pulled her hand free from the bale of hay. He pushed her hand down through her legs and placed it on his hard penis. "You are lucky, Maris'. Feel how big it is. Hold it and put it inside; I want you to do it yourself."

She was about to faint. She wanted to faint but she couldn't let it happen. With all her strength she kicked her foot behind her to find his groin.

"I'm used to kicking animals." It was an ugly laugh as he pushed himself deeply inside her. He entered her again and again. Each time she screamed. He entered her harder until she stopped screaming and he dropped to the straw, pulling her firmly on top of him. He spun her around so she was kneeling, her legs spread, across his pumping body. Her head went back, vaguely she heard him cry out and then she was tossed, sobbing onto the ground.

"Get dressed, Maris'. I will ride Scorpio over the outside show course today. At tomorrow's lesson you will see, he be faultless." He stood over her, closed his trousers and called to Dusty. "Come to the tack room after you clean yourself. You owe me for a month's lessons; we arrange your purchase of Scorpio. No more questions". He left the barn.

With strangled sobs, Marisa jumped to her feet and put her cloths over her sore, trembling body. Only one thought kept her from loosing her sanity. Tomorrow she'd make her first payment for Scorpio - a down payment for independence. Never would she tell Warren or anyone what had happened - that she had been raped. *"OH MY GOD, RAPED"* She couldn't admit it to herself. To ignore such a violation would be the most difficult thing she'd ever done, but doing it was better than giving up all she'd accomplished at Hamil Farm. John Hamil was still in control. But one day, she swore, she'd find his Achilles heel. From this moment revenge would be her constant preoccupation.

CHAPTER 6

It was already two thirty. Brad looked at his watch for the third time in fifteen minutes and paced the floor of the small apartment, running his fingers through his thick hair. *'Where the hell was Marisa?"* He worried about her riding those horses and his anxiety increased as he looked forward to seeing her. He was afraid to tell her that he loved her, he warned himself that being loved gives a woman power, loving makes her insecure. During a relationship - a love affair, there is a period where each is equally lover and beloved. That is the beautiful time - before one confesses love to the other. Then it becomes a power play, at least that is how it had been for him over the years. Once a woman told him she loved him his desire was cooled; it became an obligation - she was looking for a commitment. He wanted no more of marriage. Or so he thought. It wasn't that way with Marisa; there was something evasive about her. Even during the closest intimacies there was a mystery to her, a part of her he couldn't possess and wanted - had to have.

He looked about the room. So much of her was there. Her tennis gear was in the closet. The bow and arrows he had bought for her were in the corner, zipped neatly in a leather carrying case; he pictured her concentration as she pulled back the taut bowstring and, as if in a trance, let the arrow fly putting it in the yellow most of the time. It astounded him how directed her mind was. Brad had a secret dread that something might take her away from him.

Marisa was sickened and confused but she was finished crying, only hate burned her eyes. All the fiends of Hell were screaming in her ears, driving her out of her senses. Her brain swirled with only one thought – to get away. During the trip home she enforced her silence. What grew inside her was something stronger than humility and shame. She tried to think of her position as a wife – a woman who had been to Hell, all her integrity burnt away, a woman who would hide the scar in her heart forever. She was no more principled than John Hamil, and no less depraved with her self-righteous justification of an affair. She would not see Brad again, grateful for the cell-phone she sent him a text: '*Sorry, can't be there. M.*' Warren was all that mattered; she had no right to his love. She was a thing most foul – living a lie, defiling their marriage. There was no telling what her husband would do were he to find out. She would never speak of the desecration in the barn that had cleaved her life into 'before and after'. She had been raped. Never, never could a woman tell her man that she had been so violated and not expect him to protect his masculinity; it was the most-vile personal attack; it was a dignity that had to be restored at any cost, to the death if need be. Warren was a quietly, dangerous man.

Her mind went flying back to her first glimpse of Warren's temper before they were married. It was at a basketball victory party the last year she was in college. Donny Balfor had cut in while they were dancing. Donny was captain of The Cougars basketball team - the 'big man' on campus. He could be seen about Charleston College, a colorful cashmere sweater thrown over his shoulders, tall and pompous. He'd been named "Athlete of the Year" for his high scores and strategic leadership. Warren told him to "get lost." Later, when Marisa went upstairs to the ladies' room, Donny grabbed her and put her against the wall and kissed her. His lips traveled down her neck to the open button of her blouse. He was drunk. Marisa managed to push him away but not before Warren had come looking for her. His jaw tightened and his lips lost color in rage. They left immediately. When Donny went outside he found all four of his tires slashed, and a gash in the paint the length of his new Mercedes sports car. The next day there was unsavory gossip about the Captain of the Cougars using cocaine in the locker room. Gossip escalated to scandal, and by the end of the week the team had replaced their first Center player and chosen another Captain. Donny was retired from the team. Warren was a quietly dangerous man.

***

Home, unconscious of getting there, she went directly to the bathroom, locked the door, and threw her underwear in the wastebasket. Finally, under the scalding shower, she scrubbed and scoured her body, frantic to be cleansed of what was of John Hamil. '*Raped*'. She had been raped. Bile rose in her mouth. Careful to keep her back to the mirror not to see her image, she put on leggings and a sweat shirt and covered herself in a long flannel robe. Hamil vilified her and she vilified herself by succumbing to her ego. Need and hate, one fortified the other. One day it would be over, so buried in denial that it would be erased from her mind. But not yet. As in The Hunt, hounds are frenzied by scent, so is revenge stoked by remembrance. And, she would never tell Warren. Why should she? She rationalized. She was not guilty; it was not of her doing; she was a victim. There would be no trial, no judge and jury to give him his just due; her fury was insatiable. He would pay and it would be on her own terms, at her time, and by her own means. Marisa knew the rule that governs war: sheath your anger, know your enemy, know his thought pattern, choose your battlefield, then strike. Warren's words, his father's 'gift' extended to her.

But now she craved sleep. Those disembodied white hands haunted her.

77

***

Warren woke her when he came home. She refused dinner, saying she was unusually tired. Warren knew his wife: this was not characteristic of Marisa. She looked like a hurt, frightened animal burrowed in a dark hole. "Did something happen today?" He spoke softly, and sat on the edge of the bed to touch her cheek.

She cringed. All her skin felt wired. She wanted so much to lie in his protective arms, the arms that meant safety and home. But to be near another, to feel even the sheet against her - any sensation, made her curl up tighter to protect herself. "No, nothing happened, I'm tired – just want to sleep." She wondered how long she would be able to deny his desire.

He rubbed the back of her neck.
"Warren, please." Her head was deep in the pillow.

"I'm here, Darling." He hadn't seen her so withdrawn. Or, maybe it was himself needing the closeness of his wife. Maybe it was rejection that hurt him - woke him up to the emptiness in his life that only Marisa - only his *wife* could fill.

Blessedly, he let her go back to a fitful sleep and didn't wake her in the morning before he left.

She stayed in bed the following day. By the time she got up and began to prepare dinner she was able to deny that the violence had occurred. It was self-preservation. But only as she was cutting the salad did she recall that when she rushed back to her car at Hamil Farm, she found that she had left her keys in the door lock and her journal was on the seat with dusty fingerprints on the leather cover.

Dinner that evening was a silent formality. Although Marisa had prepared his favorite pot roast, Warren didn't taste it. Television never held his interest and he buried himself in the current automotive publications until he gave up, turned out the light on his side of the double bed and pretended to sleep.

"What is it, Warren?" Asked Marisa, softly. By disallowing her own suffering, she recognized his.

"I can't sleep, too wound up, I guess." He said, facing away from her.

"Warren." She kissed and rubbed his head. He moved away.

She knew him well; her husband would never disclose any sign of weakness.

"What is it? We can work it out together. We've always been strong, the two of us."

After a thoughtful moment he answered in a whisper. "I had a meeting with Chez at the bank today. We're selling all the property on The Neck. No more building of Raittown."

"So, we'll cut back our expenses. You'll get started somewhere else."

He stared through the darkened window. "Do you really think so? This is all I know. Raittown has become my image. It's who I am. When it's gone, I feel I'll be gone."

"Warren, everything is possible if you don't give up. You aren't 'Raittown'. Raittown is something you made. You'll create something else." Warren had asked her opinion of jobs before, but this was different. He was asking her, as if her judgement was all that mattered, to access him as a man. Lately, he rarely allowed her to know the human part of him and was always unreceptive to the deeper disclosures of marriage: the personal sorrows as well as joys.

CHAPTER 7

Wednesday morning and she hadn't been to Hamil
Farm in three days. She wanted to take her lesson
but was afraid to go alone. As was his pattern,
Warren was up early, but had nowhere to go.
Marisa gathered her courage and said: "I'm having
a private lesson today. Would you come? I'd like
you to see how well I'm doing."

Warren had no desire to go to Hamil Farm;
he didn't think what she was doing was safe, but he
decided that if he loved his wife he should show it
with more than words that say one thing and actions
that speak of another. "Sure, as soon as you're
ready."

And Marisa raced to get dressed, thrilled
that Warren would be there to share her glory.

They left the house early and stopped for
breakfast at a dinner. Warren had made a decision
about the sale of The Neck property. He would take
a loss, but he'd have credit and will-power which
were all he needed to start again. All that remained
was to sign the papers with his attorney. Marisa
saw that he was happier and he looked better too, as
people do when they pull themselves from the trap

of uncertainty and move securely forward. He held Marisa's hand as they drove toward Camden.

Marisa had never been to Hamil Farm so early but she was certain a farmer's day started at sun-up. The morning's work in the barns was always long finished by the time she arrived. She didn't ever want to meet Hamil alone again. She hoped when he saw her that he would resume his role as the rigid instructor she had esteemed. She had learned her horrid lesson and chose to store it away in her mind until she was ready to use her hatred. How sweet it would be, but now she must be silent and patient. Patient, for to act upon it now would be to forfeit all she had achieved. She would be a winner and to accomplish that she must use John Hamil.

Warren parked the Jeep in the area overlooking the large field where Hamil, Bensen and Rose-Marie were working with Cinnamon.

They remained in the car watching the workout. Cinnamon was having difficulty with the high fence. Time after time, Rose-Marie took the mare over and with each attempt the horse knocked the rail with her back hooves. Hamil and Bensen held opposite ends of the cross-pole while Rose-Marie approached the hurdle. As the horse's front legs went over, the pole was hoisted upward crashing into her belly. Cinnamon bellowed in pain. Again, Hamil repeated the punishing exercise and Marisa heard the high-pitched protest. Equating what she saw to Scorpio's mysterious injury, she got out of the car without explanation to Warren, and ran down onto the field. It was as if an unearthly blast of hot wind stopped her as three heads turned to glare at the intruder. Not a word was spoken. Bensen and Hamil reset the pole even higher than it had been on the troublesome jump. Rose-Marie brought Cinnamon faultlessly over the hurdle.

"She be fine," Marisa heard him say as his little daughter dismounted. Hamil walked up the hill to the spot where Marisa stood rooted.

"Mr. Hamil, Mr. Hamil," she called, running behind him. Mr. Hamil…"

He continued walking. Between them was no acknowledgment of what had occurred in the barn.

"Is that what happened to Scorpio? Is that how he got the bruise on his belly?"

While the words tumbled out, she saw the muscles in his neck swell and pulsate; rage came into his face over which he quickly slipped a smile that was more terrible than the anger. They exchanged a measured silent look. Gratefully, his contorted features gave way to an expression of benign composure.

"Get ready for your lesson, Maris'. I be back in fifteen minutes." He kept on with his bobbling gait into the barn.

Marisa stood a moment. What Hamil did with his horses was none of her business; she had been well informed. She had told herself that she would remain quiet and now she had broken her first rule. Marisa walked up the hill, asked Warren to wait for her, and continued into the cavernous building. It took a while for her eyes to become accustomed to the gloom. When they did she saw Hamil; he was in the tack room, absorbed in checking equipment for the upcoming show.

"Good morning, Maris'." He greeted her, warm and friendly, touching his gloved hand to the brim of his hat, as if it were the first time he had seen her that morning. "We gonna do the private lesson outside today."

"It's not too slippery with the rain?" The words escaped before she could check herself.

"Maris' if you want to hunt you have to be able to ride in all ground conditions."

She nodded and swallowed hard; her mouth was dry as she took her saddle and bridle from its place on the rack, put the tack on Scorpio, mounted, and led him outside. Warren waved and followed her down onto the field.

It had rained heavily the night before. The sky was overcast. The trampled grass was slick. Hamil had told her many times the dangers of wet grass. Yet she had seen his daughter ride Cinnamon on that wet turf. She trotted Scorpio onto the path noting with distress the effort the horse required to pull his feet from the mud. Scorpio wanted his head. To settle him, she allowed him to run slowly. They practiced changing leads. Marisa looked over at the split rail fence. Hamil was by the post.

Scorpio knew the course well; he had been schooled there. They took the fence easily and the brush box. They came off the coop. Water burst from the ground beneath his hooves. Marisa wasn't sure if it were she or Scorpio the teacher was instructing. At his command, John Hamil could get a precision performance from the greenest horse. She turned to make a wide approach to the final barrier – the stack of massive tree trunks protruding atop a grassy knoll. Hamill was there.

Scorpio galloped straight on.

Marisa set herself against her own judgement that prompted her to stop. Fear became an elixir. She must remember all she had been taught. She gave Scorpio the signal, felt the horse collect himself beneath her, bunching his muscles, straining forward. She was in perfect position: off the withers, chin thrust forward, a surge of power from the hindquarters and they crossed the pinnacle in unison. It was then that Marisa saw the grin on John Hamil's face and knew terror. Scorpio's front feet touched down and skidded from beneath him. He somersaulted heavily to the ground. In the engulfing blackness there was only that face. It would have been a nightmare but Marisa knew it was not a dream. Full consciousness evaded her as she floundered in limbo between two hells. Comforting warmth spread across her face and neck; she didn't know it was her blood. All was blackness, there was no sound; all she knew was that Warren was holding her.

***

Along with the mail adding to the clutter on Rob MacGrath's desk was a package the size of a shoebox wrapped in brown, paper tied with a string. He would have given it to his secretary to open but that it appeared so child-like, and was marked personal. There was no return address. 'Just another sample or gift from a solicitor', he reasoned and pushed the package aside until after he met his deadline for the final edit of tomorrow's paper. An hour later the presses were rolling; he cut the string, tore off the paper and opened the box. "Ahh!" He cried and knocked it off the desk. It bumped the metal wastebasket and dropped onto the floor with a soft thud. Unable to believe his eyes, he peered over the desktop. A huge decapitated rat rolled out from a page of newspaper. Though much was blackened by dried blood he was able to make-out the by-line: '*Leslie Allen*'. He comprehended immediately. "Hamil. Somehow Hamil had found out about the story. But how would he know that Marisa was *Leslie Allen*? No, possibly it wasn't Hamil and had nothing to do with Marisa." He was being irrational. "It was just another jokester, a random piece of newspaper." But years as a newspaperman taught him that truth is worse than what could be imagined. Immediately, he called Marisa at home. After four endless rings, he was greeted by an automated message. He hung up, tried her cell phone. No answer. Once more he tried the two phone numbers to no avail. '*Wait an hour and try again,*' he told himself, aware that he was becoming paranoid, never-the-less, he telephoned the Police

Station in Camden and inquired if there had been a reported accident to Marisa Rait.

"Let me pull up the list." The officer said.

Mac pictured him in front of his computer with a long list of names from all over the county.

"No. I see no, *Marisa Rait.* But…." His voice dragged. "I see there was an ambulance dispatched to a riding stable - Hamil Farm, at nine eighteen this morning. I don't have a name of the victim as yet."

"What hospital?" He snapped.

"Memorial."

The drive up the Mark Clark Expressway to Camden's Memorial Hospital was mechanical - the accelerator pressed to the floor. With the formidable determination of the quarterback he once was, Mac darted through the traffic that blocked him. *'Marisa? An accident? No'.* When you stalk and corner an animal or a human he becomes dangerous. So it was with Hamil and Mac blamed himself for what happened.

Since the day Marisa began riding with John Hamil, the editor had feared for her. Anyone else would have done a regular reporting job, but Marisa - she had to live it. *'An Accident?'* So vague and meaningless a word. *'Dear God'*, it was no accident. He crashed through the door of the ER where he saw Warren, tense and ashen. "Marisa?"

"I saw her fall." His voice was hollow.

A door swung open. "Mr. Rait, I'm Dr. Ostin." His solemn voice was barely audible.

"A fall, Warren, a fall?" Mac asked. Both men ignored him.

The doctor was speaking to Warren quickly as if to be rid of a childish nuisance, "She's lost a lot of blood and her nervous system is in trauma. It was a severe concussion. There is no skull fracture. We've got her stabilized but we'll have to wait until she wakes up to tell the extent of her injuries. We'll know more in twenty-four hours."

"Dr. Ostin. Dr. Ostin." A clinical voice came over the intercom. He nodded uncomfortably, patted Warren gently on the shoulder and stared down the corridor.

It was all Warren could do to control his temper. "Take me to my wife. Let me see her." His wanted to take the infuriatingly calm man by the collar. His wife was not simply an hour out of a surgeon's occupational day.

An orderly took Warren's arm and led him through the ER doors, passing Rob MacGrath as if he were invisible.

Marisa lay unconscious inside a florescent-lighted cubicle. Her still body looked small beneath the sheet on the railed bed. Above was a flashing machine, which emitted beeping noises. There were bruises and swelling around her eyes; her breathing was shallow. The right side of her head was wrapped in a large bandage. Her face was pale as the pillowcase on which her mud matted hair spread. The room smelled antiseptic. A nurse opened the curtain, nudged Warren aside, checked the blood pressure and the blood that was dripping intravenously into Marisa's arm and stepped out.

Warren didn't speak. Words of emotion between he and his wife had been few. He believed being there was enough; just lately, he learned that love needs reassuring. He touched the still fingers and stood by her for a long moment; then turned, leaving the ugly green room with its ugly sounds and smells. He had to get control of the situation. If he didn't he wondered if he could go on living. He fell back on instinct. By instinct Warren was a problem solver - a businessman. Medicine was a business and he would get the best in that business.

Marisa was crushed under what seemed an unfathomable weight and unspeakable pain that she did not feel but was conscious of. Every so often words drifted down; they were audible and out of context.

"Mr. Rait."

"They all…."

"We don't know, Mr. Rait. She…"

She could hardly breath. She opened her eyes and looked up. Faces swam far, very far above, just below a shimmering brightness that had to be the surface. She saw Warren. His features were strained. Something terrible had happened. She tried to call to him, to reach out to him but she was so tired and so far away; he didn't hear her and stepped out of the brightness.

There were other faces - bored faces; she didn't like them. She closed her eyes.

Marisa remained in the hospital for three weeks. Warren was there throughout the day and slept on a cot at her bedside each night until she gained full consciousness. MacGrath, also, was there, but she was hardly aware of them. There was only the constant pain in her back and a maelstrom in her head. The sickening dizzy spells she was told would pass. Her left leg was weak from trauma to her spinal cord. The doctors doubted if she would be able to walk. This was unacceptable. With will-power and physical therapy she strengthened the muscles and surprised them all. Marisa could tolerate the physical pain but mental pain ate into her heart and altered her being.

'Time. It altered life in a flash. How strange was time.' She spent every conscious moment constructing in her mind the article she would write about Hamil Farm. She asked Warren to bring her her journal, but she needed no reference.

It wasn't until the last night she was in the hospital that she thought of Brad. She called him late, near midnight, well after Warren left.

"Marisa, thank God!"
At the sound of his voice she began to cry. She told him what had happened.

"Where are you? I'm coming."

"No, no. I don't want you to see me this way. It's not the same. I'm not the same. What we had cannot be part of my life". There was remorse in her voice but conviction was stronger.

If only he could see her, hold her close, she would see nothing had changed. Nothing could change the way he felt, the way they were together. "Just tell me where you are. When you didn't come that afternoon, I called Hamil Farm; the woman said you weren't there. There was no answer at your house."

Her heart plunged down to her stomach. "My house? How did you get my number? It's not listed."

"MacGrath's secretary. I told her I had lost it. She saw us together at the office, she assumed we knew each-other".

"Brad you shouldn't have called my house. How could you?" Caution alerted her; she dried her tears.

"When you didn't come, I didn't know what to think."

"I wouldn't just leave you. Brad, please try to understand. I'm sorry, I just can't see you again. What I did was wrong. I'm sorry. I'm sorry." She was sobbing again.

"Marisa, I love you." For the first time he said the words. "I love you." He said them as a pledge that he would exchange his protective solitude for her love. But his willingness only met rejection. She hung up without a reply.

The sickly green walls closed around her; she cried for what wrong she had done to Warren and to Brad and she cried for herself.

Mac tried to dissuade her from writing the article. 'Sweet, silent Mac' told her not to write it for to relive it would be painful. He told her that he would write the article himself as he had been writing the *Leslie Allen* column for weeks - since she was in the hospital. He didn't want to risk its sudden absence which could shed suspicion on her. But Mac didn't understand that pain is necessary to make truth jump from the page. She wanted others who had also suffered with John Hamil to know they weren't alone and he was no longer free of scrutiny.

MacGrath had brought the box with the decapitated rat to the police and told them he thought Hamil had sent it, that somehow Hamil was the cause of Marisa's fall.

They didn't buy the story. 'There is no proof and no motive. Hamil has nothing to hide. It was an accident.' They said. "Her husband was there. He was a witness. She fell. Horseback riding is dangerous. And jumping? That's foolish. Anyone who jumps has had an accident. Ask any member of The Hunt. They all have stories of broken bones."

But no words of logic could dissuade him. MacGrath was convinced that it was Hamil who sent the threat and he felt responsible. Marisa, he noticed, had changed. She'd developed a way of receiving information without revealing how she digested it. She made no comment about the box when he told her. She no longer spoke of Hamil. She didn't blame anyone. She just wrote the truth – fact by fact.

Mystery, Rob MacGrath believed, is a source of strength. Marisa striped Hamil of that weapon. She wrote candidly of all she had seen and endured at Hamil Farm so that anyone who read the words would see what lay behind the masterful image. She wrote of cruelty to animals and to the human spirit and of his disregard of safety, even that of his own young daughter. Marisa spat all the venom from her body onto the page.

The article was on MacGrath's desk and ready for publication before she left the hospital.

He refused to print it. "Enough harm has been done". He told her. "Y'know he is capable of anything and we can't accuse him without proof. The police call what happened to you an accident. Leave it alone. Stay away from Hamil."

"Print it, Mac. Print it." She insisted.
He did.

***

The newspapers sold out. The article was whispered about in silken parlors, in coffee shops, at the bars, and at The Hunt Club dinners where John Hamil was no longer welcome. People began to talk of past incidents: injuries to their horses or their safety put in jeopardy. The equestrian community is tight. News traveled up and down the eastern seaboard. *Leslie Allen* became a hero. The public speculated if the reporter was male or female. They knew that the informer must be a regular at Hamil Farm however suspicion never fell on the newcomer - Marisa Rait. Then, as scandal goes, the whispering stopped.

She wasn't able to go home. She couldn't climb the stairs to her front door without help and the dizzy spells persisted. Her left leg was weak and she walked with a cane. Warren knew she wouldn't be able to drive the Jeep; the stiff clutch would be impossible. He sold the SUV to Chez, though he refused to retire his old truck. They moved into her father's house, to the bedroom on the ground floor. Marisa never thought she'd be back living in that house with her parents but Warren didn't want her to be alone until the dizziness passed.

"I've always taken care of myself. Are you trying to make me an invalid while you go about your business?"

Warren grimaced at her misjudgment. "I want you never to forget this ordeal and I want you to be very cautious not to injure yourself again. Nerves don't heal a second time." He kissed her cheek and left the house.

She had never spoken like that to Warren and didn't mean the cruel words. She was lashing out at the one in the world she loved most and he stood up to her, not taking to heart what she said. She should have had such trust, and insight. Now, she blamed herself but at the time she felt he deserted her and she put her trust in Brad and in John Hamil; his praise was essential. Strange, this habit of hers, transferring total trust from one person to another for a completely different reason.

It was total need. It was selfish and came as a painful lesson - it was herself she must trust solely.

Fortunately, her mother hadn't changed. She was still occupied with her social schedule and did no more than whirl past with a list of warnings and criticisms. Her father was delighted she was there. They went for long, slow walks, which made her stronger. As in her childhood, they read together in the sun and quoted passages from the classic novels they adored. This beautiful part of her life she felt defined her. But that was *before*, before Hamil, before the ugliness of vengeance.

At the end of each day she was on the verandah waiting for Warren. When he came home she'd pour his Bourbon and look at it greedily while sipping iced tea. Then he might take her shopping and wait while she tried on and modeled a new dress. To buy the dress for her made him happy. They'd have dinner together - sometimes out, sometimes in the house with her parents at the mahogany table under the crystal chandelier, while two maids served.

For Warren life at the Lawner household had an order that he liked. He always knew where Marisa was and that she was safe. He was sorry when she stated that she was ready to go back to her own house.

Marisa was vain and brawny now, her pain having given birth to a new energy. She walked straight and held her head high with only an ebony staff for support. She and Warren bought it at one of the antique stalls in the Old Slave Market. The handle was a silver viper's head. It possessed a cold beauty that has deceived man since his creation. Marisa abhorred snakes but regarded the staff as a symbol that this too, she would overcome.

On Valentine's Day Warren surprised her with a Corvette - a red Corvette.

***

Ellen Coleman watched with peculiar sorrow as Bensen herded the six horses into the old van. Scorpio was the last. No one had told her that Mr. Hamil was selling Scorpio to those sleazy carpetbagger types from Florida. With so many horses in that state, it made no sense for them to come North only to drive down a vanload of horses. Ellen felt lonely at Hamil Farm without Marisa. Those that remained neither asked about her or mentioned her name. She was glad that her husband had built a barn in their back yard.

Larry was a general sales manager of a department store chain and was away from the house five days a week. *'Someone should be available for the children.'* Larry explained. Having the barn at home, she could still continue her lessons with Hamil. It meant towing London Fog two miles in her rig but she'd be gaining time at home where she could work the horse in her own corral. Ellen saw the glow of his constant cigarette

as he turned into the driveway of Hamil Farm with
the new horse trailer to take London Fog to his new
home just as the rickety truck pulled out carrying
Scorpio.

John Hamil stood watching by the upstairs window
of the frame house and smiled satisfactorily as the
van departed. He then returned to the sink to finish
his ritual shave. This hour, between seven and eight
o'clock on Sunday mornings, was his alone. The
barn jobs had been attended to earlier and there
were no lessons until after noon. His gaze was
fixed on his reflection. No one, he was certain,
perceived it but he saw that each wrinkle in the
careful planning of his affairs affected his
appearance. Once a week he would lock the door
of the small bedroom and erase the image of the
humble farmer. Shaved and showered, whether
Hunt Season or Show season, he donned the attire
of the *chasseur:* tall gleaming black boots, and red
Hunt coat with polished brass buttons. Carefully,
he unwrapped the crinkling tissue paper from his
black silk top hat and adjusted it on his head. He
noticed approvingly that the irritating threadlike
furrows that had crept from his nose to his mouth
were now smooth. '*Scorpio was finally off the
grounds.*' He complimented himself for putting the
deed to Hamil Farm in his wife's name, making any
personal liability suit against him virtually
uncollectable. Warren Rait would soon discover

that students come to Hamil Farm at their own assumption of risk.

Long ago, Hamil found that as an alien in a strange country he could feign ignorance and thereby manipulate the insurance companies. He'd stash the money when the premium was paid on the six dead horses.

"Too bad." He could hear the adjuster's sympathetic tone. "Who would have foreseen a truck breakdown and the poor animals dehydrating within its hot confines? We're sorry, Mr. Hamil. A shame the driver couldn't get them water."

The horses were legally his until delivered to the ranch in Florida, therefore he would be covered for the loss. He postured back and forth around the four-poster bed. The insurance money would cover the exorbitant costs of running the International Junior Equestrian show circuit with Rose-Marie. High entry fees and traveling expenses across the United States and Europe with a string of horses were prohibitive to the families of many young riders. Hamil never let anything stand in his way. Rose-Marie Hamil would be champion in the image of her father. And, what a victory it would be, with the finals being held that summer in Brussels. That city would never again forget the name Hamil. Rose-Marie was his means. In Brussels, as in New York's Madison Square Garden, he would reinforce the name "Hamil" to be synonymous with "Champion." No one would ever call John Hamil *"Boy."*

CHAPTER 8

The laundry was hanging on the line drying in the April sun. It had been more than a week since she had received a letter from Rose-Marie, but each day Margaret Hamil prepared for its arrival. The mailman came at eleven in the morning. By that time she made sure the kitchen was spotless. She wanted everything neat and orderly so when the letter did come she could sit down quietly at her table to read without the nagging impulse to finish a chore. Since her husband and Rose-Marie left on the show circuit she adhered to the pattern so that at this time she could hang her apron on its peg in the pantry, and go upstairs.

She put on a fresh dress, always conscious of the little bulges that appeared as cushions on her hips. Since she had turned forty, and that was five years ago, she was dismayed to have to let out the seams on all her dresses. She fixed the brown braids atop her head, put a dab of powder on her nose and pinched her pale cheeks. After two decades in America, Margaret Hamil still held firmly to all appearances and household customs of a Flemish peasant woman. At eleven twenty-five she was in the front yard so she could see the postman when he came. He was waving a striped edged airmail envelope as he trod up the drive.

"Oh, thank God." She breathed, remaining taciturn, her face placid; they exchanged cordialities. Then she walked slowly into the house, set the letter on the table and pulled out her chair, smoothing her skirt as she sat. The letter was postmarked Madrid, Spain, April 10, one week ago:

Dear Mama,

I miss you. I wish I had some yummy griddlecakes like we had for breakfast the day Papa and I left. Me and this kid, Geoffrey Kent, he's from a town near London and veddy British, are tied on points. Everyone treats Papa nicely and he's okay. They just don't talk to him too much. He makes me go to bed early and get up early. I keep up with my studies after dinner. The other kids my age go out together in the evening before dinner, but he won't let me go. He says we are here to work. He bought me a pretty doll with long hair like mine. I brush her hair before I go to sleep like you brush mine. Daddy brushes it for me now. When I get home I want to go to the movies and see my friends. All I've done is travel from city to city in America and now country to country in Europe. There is another show every few days. I practice in the mornings, then I eat and then I sleep. We have so many ribbons, Mama. At first I thought it was fun, but now I'm tired, Mama and want to come home to you. Next week is the finals in Brussels; probably

*as you are reading this letter I am in the last show.
Papa watches me every minute. I have to win for
him, Mama. Do you understand? Next time you see
me I'll be a champion like Papa. Won' t that be
good?*

> *Love and Kisses,*
> *Rose-Marie*

Margaret reread her daughter's letter for the third
time and caressed the familiar block printing as if it
were Rose-Marie's soft cheek. She hurt inside. *'It
wasn't proper to put a little girl in that competition
so she felt she had to win for him, it wasn't proper
that he had taken her out of school.'* It was no more
proper now than it had been two years ago when
Rose-Marie had fallen from Atta Boy. She
remembered the fear welling in her chest as she ran
to her daughter, the warm blood that flowed freely
over her hands from the gaping wound on Rose-
Marie's forehead. It was cause for Margaret to
promise herself not to let any further harm befall
her child. And now that promise was broken
because she was weak and silent. She was forced to
remain silent though her heart cried out to stop him
when he told her he was taking Rose-Marie on tour.
Her husband's look, as she opened her mouth in
protest, struck her as forcefully as a whiplash and
once more Margaret was reduced to servitude and
cowered in silence.

She had never felt at ease in America.
Flanders was her home, and she hadn't been there

since she and John left so quickly twenty years ago. To have been rejected from the Belgian Olympic Team was not a disgrace in her eyes and the failure didn't warrant stealing away from your home with what few possessions you could carry. However, Margaret was brought up in the ways of the old country. She was a good Christian and honored her husband. It was an arranged marriage; her place was at his side. Margaret read the letter again, folded it carefully and put it in the shoebox with Rose-Marie's other letters. She never imagined that time could move so slowly without her child playing around the house and working in the kitchen with her. Even now, with the promise of Rose-Marie's triumph in reach, she felt sad and lost and had taken to staying within the security of the house. Margaret tried to avoid Bensen. He was always around, not talking, but spying on her, she thought while vigorously polishing the silver tea service she had brought on that voyage from Belgium. It was all she could take being crammed in 'steerage', below deck next to the engine room with so many sweaty, noise- deafened immigrants. Whenever she was uneasy, she polished that silver, though she had never used it. She planned to set it out in all its splendor when John and Rose-Marie came home at the end of the month. By that time, she would have finished the organdy curtains and bedspread she was sewing for Rose-Marie's bedroom. *'What a wonderful surprise it will be.'* And John, she knew, would be pleased with the three colts that were now strong and frolicking in the pasture. All will be well soon, Margaret told herself and rubbed the silver teapot more briskly.

***

BRUSSELS, BELGIUM

The final event of the long contest that would give international recognition as Junior Equestrian Champion to an entrant of ten to sixteen years of age was underway. All seats in the Coliseum were taken and standing room had been sold out. People in the dress circle were in formal attire and teen-age fans, in jeans and sweatshirts, pressed against the high balconies for a better view. Flags of all nations hung motionless from the rafters around the perimeter of the theater that was flooded with artificial sunlight. The red and gold uniformed orchestra finished playing.

Eight youngsters came into the arena. Each, in his own manner, walked the course, stamping the ground with their boots and counting the strides between obstacles. When they were satisfied with their knowledge and the condition of the course they walked out. Moments later a rider appeared. There was a respectful hush. The horse passed through a swinging gate.

Inside the paddock area ten-year-old Rose-Marie Hamil shivered at the sound of the starting buzzer. She would be the last rider in the Jump-off.

"Stop fidgeting and be still. Cinnamon will sense your nervousness." Her father snapped.

"I'm sorry, Papa." It had been an exhausting, hard-pressed two months and the tension showed in the youngster's pinched, colorless face.

"Cinnamon is the best in this timed course over fences. Remember, style is not scored; it's speed and accuracy. He be fine. Keep the reins slack and lean forward over his neck."

"Yes, Sir." She said and bit her lip as she counted the buzzers.

He straightened the white stock tie at her neck and secured her hard velvet hunt cap over the coiled bun he had made of her hair. "Mount up, Rose-Marie, you be next. After this, we go home." He helped her into the saddle, checked the girth, secured her feet in the irons and patted her knee. "Win, Rose-Marie. You be champion, sure."

Cinnamon trotted into the arena. Rose-Marie had never seen such an awesome crowd, such pomp and attentiveness. The little girl turned to look back at her father, her eyes all the bluer by the royal blue hacking jacket she wore. He nodded with proud assurance. Rose-Marie pressed her knees gently to the horse's flank. They cantered, and then galloped easily in a circle. They were ready. She turned the horse to the jump course, passing through the stanchions with the electric eyes. The buzzer started the clock. Seconds ticked on. There was a series of eight hurdles, all of them she managed faultlessly. Cinnamon took the last fence and passed through the gates to stop the running time. It was a perfect course, executed in record time. The audience rose and applauded wildly. The lathered horse was confused and pulled on the bit. A boy jumped in front of the winded child and flashed a camera at the new Junior International Equestrian Champion. Blinded and frightened, Cinnamon reared high on her hind legs, flayed at the air and fell over on her back. Silence. There was a split second of stunned immobility before grooms rushed out to pull the fallen horse off the rider. Rose-Marie was dead before the ambulance reached the hospital.

The International News Service published the picture-story of pretty, little Rose-Marie Hamil, daughter of the once famous John Hamil, who carried the title home to her mother in an insignificant wooden box, which also contained her small broken body.

***

Warren and Marisa were having breakfast on the verandah enjoying the early Spring day. They had moved back into their own home. Though the dizzy spells persisted, they were less frequent, and if Marisa was careful not to turn her head quickly she could control them. In that way she was able to enjoy the Corvette on local streets. She would drive around the neighborhood and stop outside the deli where she used to shop. The owner would bring her a sandwich, which she took to a spot overlooking the river and have her lunch in the car. It was so good to be alone, without people watching her every move out of the corner of their eye. But, today, she wouldn't go back there. Not after yesterday. While watching the boats pass under the bridge, she had noticed a man walking toward her: long strides, a familiar swagger, longish brown hair pushed behind his ears, aviator sunglasses. *'Brad? No, it couldn't be Brad.'* Her heart beat quickened. She tried to see his face clearly as he neared but then he turned and went off in the opposite direction. *'It couldn't be Brad.'* And she appreciated, once more, his respect for her request not to see her again. Instead of finishing her sandwich, she started the engine and hurried home.

Warren finished his orange juice and stood up from the table. "I don't like Monday mornings. In my next life I think I'll be a housewife and sit in the sun all day." He laughed as he stretched and picked up his worn briefcase.

"Is that what you think I do with my time?" Marisa taunted holding his arm and walking down the stairs to the garage.

"What are your plans today, Darling?" She looked particularly lovely this morning in black linen trousers and a black T-shirt with a black cashmere cardigan tied around her waist. The serpentine walking stick accessorized the outfit dramatically. There was an intriguing new depth to her beauty he couldn't define.

A decisive silence, then: "I thought I'd drive up to visit Ellen Coleman." She met his eyes, looked away quickly.

"Marisa, haven't we finished with horses?"

"I am Warren. Ellen is my friend. I'd like to spend some time with her."

"I'm happy for you to see Ellen but it's too dangerous for you to drive on the Freeway."

"I know you think so; my father will take me."

"Your father? How did you arrange that?"

"He wants to drive the Corvette."

"I won't stop you." He yanked up the garage door to reveal his Honda in the space that had previously been occupied by the Jaguar. "But you know I don't like you going out there." The signs were subtle but he noticed she was pushing to get out and about on her own. Since the accident he had been part of everything she did, even to helping her into the bath and drying her off. He liked her dependence. She had been thrilled to see her strength improving, and looked to him as the miracle worker never questioning his judgement. Yet, it was really she, he confessed to himself, who had brought him a new happiness and turned him away from his inward nature. It came to Warren how strong his wife really was. She was one of the enviable few who make things happen.

It was the first time Marisa had gone the familiar route since that January morning of the accident.

She was prepared for mixed feelings - feelings of fear or perhaps a longing. Instead, she was smiling and looked forward to seeing Ellen, as she would a friend with whom she shared an interest. Except when she thought of Brad. She had disciplined her mind not to think of him but on this road remembrance of his body, his smile, her hand in his, threatened her barricade. They passed the turn-off where she would meet him at the inn. She shuttered to believe that at one time he was so important in her life, an indulgence with no significance nor longevity. Involuntarily, she craned her neck, looking for the BMW that would be waiting under the Willow Tree by the side of the road.

"Did I pass the exit?" Her father asked seeing her stress.

"No. I was confused. It's further up. Are you enjoying the car?"

The top was down. She tied a scarf around her hair. The music was blaring.

"Makes me feel like a kid." He accelerated. "Warren was right to get this for you. It's much easier to drive than the Jeep. That clutch was hard." He was changing the radio stations. "Oh, listen to this group. They're on every station. Do you know them?"

She tightened her scarf. "*Light Year, t*hey're okay". It was one of Brad's promotions, now on The Top Ten List.

"*Galaxy*. That's the album. Your mother bought me the CD. It's more jazz than rock, don't you think? We danced to it after dinner last night".

"Would you turn it off, please? It's giving me a headache with all the wind noise." She always thought her parents lived together in tolerance for the sake of propriety; it was impossible to imagine her dear father holding his domineering wife in his arms and rocking to contemporary music. She had to assume that they had their own unique bonding. Perhaps it was trust. She had broken her covenant of trust with Warren. To think of it was to weep. This was no time for tears.

They drove on in silence until she saw the sign - *Woodside Park*. "That's it Daddy, we turn here."

Woodside Park was a development: rows of identical clapboard matchbox houses, some more elaborate than others if one counted a plastic fawn planted on the lawn. They drove down the treeless road, once lush woods mowed down by merciless tractors. It pleased Marisa to recognize Warren's superior designing of Raittown. Warren respected the trees.

"Now we look for green shutters on the left and an oversized yard. They have a double building plot." They found Ellen's #1107 Park Avenue, a decal of a horse's head adorned the mailbox.

Ellen ran out to meet them when she heard the car. She didn't know what to expect Marisa's condition to be. Her last remembrance of Marisa was a still form plugged into a life support apparatus. Much to Ellen's relief, Marisa looked as she had when they used to ride together. Cripples made her uneasy. She excused herself thinking it a throwback to the time of her own injury. She recalled her fury when heads would turn to watch her clumsy maneuver into a chair. It was her first glimpse of the aversion the perfect have for the misshapen, the carefree for the miserable. Of course there were those people who had enough discretion to look away if she met their brazen stares and a few that smiled to show their discomfort. Now she was part of that observing group.

The two girls embraced. Marisa introduced her father.

"Come on in." Ellen said. "I thought you might like some coffee. Later, I'll show you my barn. Do you like horses, Mr. Lawner?"

"I was Marisa's first riding partner."
With her father's help she managed to traverse the uneven stone path and the three stairs up to the front door. From the kitchen came the welcoming aroma of brewing coffee. They followed Ellen and sat at the Formica table, while she filled the mugs and set out a box of sugarcoated doughnuts. Marisa helped herself to milk from the soggy, half-empty carton and passed it to her father, watching with amusement his expression of disgust. Ellen's Collie rubbed against his leg and left long white hairs on his gray trousers. It was too much for the conservative financier. After giving the dog his untouched doughnut, he excused himself, walked to the sink and placed his cup beside two crushed beer cans and an open cardboard box from Tony's Pizzeria. The pie was devoured but for the crust, which had been flung back into the box. One piece had missed and lay, as mush, in a greasy frying pan.

Mr. Lawner caught Marisa's eye with a look of intolerance, assuming this was the remnants of last night's family meal. He stepped outside.

Marisa let Ellen lead the conversation covering the usual topics of children, fashion, and decorating ideas for her home. Both avoided the subject of John Hamil. Marisa looked out the window at her father by the barn, not knowing how much longer his patience would endure.

"Ellen, how is Margaret Hamil? You and she used to be friends when you kept Fog at the farm. Have you seen her since Rose-Marie's death?"

"Oh, Marisa, the woman is pathetic, so thin. She won't come out of the house. I stopped by to bring her some cookies I baked. She was sitting at the kitchen table moving her body back and forth to the droning refrigerator while she rubbed a silver teapot. A steady stream of ants were crawling from the rotted windowsill down the wall and along the baseboard; she seemed not to notice. After a while she went upstairs. I followed her into Rose-Marie's bedroom. It was filled with fresh flowers, pink and white, full of joy, waiting to give welcome. She opened the bureau drawers and touched the neatly folded clothes. She didn't say a word; she just let me look. I pray I never know the agony of a mother's loss." Ellen wiped her eyes. "He destroyed his child; next it will be his wife. I'm afraid her misery will kill her. I hear Mr. Hamil never goes to the house except to eat dinner or sleep." Ellen had said all this in one breath. "Poor Rose-Marie. She tried so hard for her father. I don't think she really wanted to go on that tour at all. She did it for him. I wonder if she did it out of love, or duty or was it fear that made her go?"

Marisa looked at her steadily. "Fear or love, they amounted to the same."

"He never mentions her name, like he never mentions your name. I think you were special to him in a weird way. I thought he was challenged by you but I didn't understand why." She poured herself another mug of coffee, went to give Marisa some, and realized her cup was full. The red light on the coffee maker flickered. "It's still hot, want a fresh cup?"

"Thanks." She feigned interest in the coffee, took a bite out of the doughnut. "How often do you go to the stables now?"

"I take my lessons twice a week. It's no trouble, really. I put Fog in the trailer; I'm there and saddled up in less than an hour. We're doing well in shows but if Fog needs help I leave him there and Mr. Hamil schools him for me. I bought a horse from him for the kids, but there's still one empty stall in the barn here. I like it this way and the kids help. They're taking lessons too. We ride together. The woods behind the house has wonderful trails."

"Ellen, you tell me he destroyed his child, he's killing his wife, you see what happened to me, and no one has to remind you of your own suffering. It escapes me why you don't see what the man is. You're obsessed with him. Find someone else."

"Come on, Marisa, he's the best. You know it. There isn't a person who knows horses or trains them better than John Hamil. Rose-Marie's tragedy is no secret and despite that scathing news article, Hamil has paying boarders who depend on him to school their horses. I'm one of them. I love my horses and I won't do anything with them without first consulting Mr. Hamil. He's strict. So what?"

"Then…" Marisa paused for emphasis, and leaning forward continued, "Why was he dismissed as head of The Hunt?"

Ellen stood up from the table. "How did you know about that?"

"My husband has a friend who rides in The Hunt. He said Hamil was dismissed, blackballed, at the request of the members Why?" In truth, it was Mac who had passed the information.

Ellen turned not to face her but not before Marisa saw that her lower lip was quivering. "They said too many people were having unnecessary accidents."

"Every one that jumps, knows if you jump horses you will eventually fall."

"But the accidents were too many and too serious. They said he pushes his riders beyond their experience and ability." She wiped powdered sugar from her mouth, sat down - stirred her coffee in an effort to look blasé, then with a change of attitude addressed Marisa. "I'm not a child nor a thrill seeker and these people who board with Hamil aren't either. It's the riding: being there, being able to lessen the difference between yourself and your horse, to bond with the horse physically and emotionally as John Hamil does, to learn a new meaning of …of freedom."

She spoke with conviction and Marisa was again able to feel the ecstasy of being on Scorpio's back, running across a field; being part of that harmony.

Ellen went on in a rush. "We all know what we're doing. Mr. Hamil doesn't make anyone do what they don't want to do or think they can't do. You can always refuse."

"Ellen, you're kidding yourself but you can't fool me. It was you who first said that Hamil takes away your reasoning. I know what John Hamil is. He's evil. If you don't believe he might cause harm to you or your children by all means continue with him. But before we close the subject, let me ask you this." Marisa scraped back her chair and stood up so Ellen would have to raise her eyes. "No one actually saw me fall that morning of the accident did they? Except Bensen and Warren, but he was far away. It was after I'd seen them pole Cinnamon. Hamil told Warren that I dropped a stirrup and fell. That's not what happened."

No longer able to sit still under Marisa's hard gaze, Ellen got up and went to the sink.

Marisa waited until she returned to her chair. They were eye to eye. "And Scorpio?"

"He was sold. Mr. Hamil sold him and a few more horses to some guys with a ranch or a plantation in Florida. I was there when they picked them up."

"It didn't seem strange to you that he would sell Scorpio, a perfectly trained school horse, good

114

to show or hunt? How long after the accident did they come?

"It was about a month later. No one wanted to ride Scorpio after you were hurt; the horse had a history of slipping."

"And Hamil knew it?"

"Oh, he knew it. Scorpio had fallen twice going over a water jump during a Hunt. Once during the Brookvale Hunt." She stopped talking abruptly, the next words hung in the air waiting to be said.

"Yes?"

"When I hurt myself. I was riding Scorpio." She looked at her hands in her lap. "That was before I bought Fog, before you came to Hamil Farm."

"You? You knew he was a '*slipper*'? Marisa exclaimed. "Why didn't you tell me? Hamil means so much to you that you would knowingly endanger a friend?"

"He would have known I told you. I was afraid."

"Afraid of what?"

"That he would tell me to leave."

There was no logic to Ellen's allegiance to John Hamil. "So, he knew Scorpio was a slipper when he told me to take the lesson outside after the rain. And that's where Scorpio is now, in Florida? Very odd, Scorpio is a gelding; they couldn't use him for stud. He wasn't the greatest show horse in the county; sure he was well schooled, but that's no reason for anyone to go through the expense and bother to van an ordinary horse like Scorpio such a distance?"

Ellen was clasping and unclasping her fingers. "They didn't have a regular horse van. They trucked him and five other horses."

"Trucked? What do you mean?"

"I was at the farm early that morning; I saw Bensen load the horses in an old truck. Hamil sold the guys those horses and they…"

"They what, Ellen?"

"They died. All the horses died." She looked down and twisted her hands.

Marisa suspected that the sale of Scorpio was other than to rid his barn of a *slipper* to insure his students' safety. "What happened? Tell me all that happened, Ellen." She insisted coolly.

"Well, the old truck broke down. Those jerks were thinking of money and must have forgotten that horses need water in the hot sun. It was in Georgia that it broke. They left the horses closed up inside the truck while they looked for a mechanic or parts or something and then they hurried to Florida. When they got there the animals were too weak to save. One was already dead in the truck."

"That bastard. That dirty bastard." She snarled. "Go on."

Ellen stammered. "I wasn't at the farm much after that. He stopped giving lessons and the next I knew he was on tour with Rose-Marie. I'm sorry, Marisa. I didn't want to tell you."

"And how did I get to the hospital after I fell?"

"Margaret called an ambulance from the house. Margaret was the only person who asked me how you were. I think she was genuinely concerned. She knew we were friends. Neither of them went to the hospital. They gave the information to the police. After that no one spoke about you. It was lonely there, Marisa. Really it was. Larry wasted no time getting the pre-fab barn erected for me; I brought Fog home, and then Mr. Hamil was gone."

The kitchen door opened with a creak. "Oh, Daddy, I forgot the time." She looked at Ellen. "Thanks for the coffee."

"If you go out that way, you'll pass the barn." Ellen indicated a side door from the kitchen.

They walked, by the white-board fence enclosing the paddock, to the red barn. Ellen slid back the door. Marisa breathed the perfume of oiled leather and sweet hay. There was an orderly tack room and four stalls: London Fog, another smaller horse, and a pony; one was empty. The barn was spic-and-span; a sharp contrast to Ellen's unkempt kitchen. Marisa had no doubt where Ellen placed her priorities.

"That's Shandi." Said Ellen, pointing to a gleaming brass nameplate. She's very quiet. She used to be a racehorse but anyone can ride her now. Hamil trained her especially for the kids but I ride her, myself, once in a while.

"Marisa, it's late." Her father said and took her by the elbow to steer her outside.

"I'll drive, Dad."

"On the Freeway? You haven't done that."

"I'm fine. I've been fine. I'll drive slowly in the right lane." She spun around, put her arms around him and kissed him. "I'm fine, Daddy, really. But the top goes up." She turned to go. "Ellen, what are you planning for the fourth stall? Is Larry going to buy another horse?"

"No. I could take a boarder, but that would be more work and then I'd have no privacy. I'll keep it empty for a while, I guess."

After they waved good-bye, Ellen turned the horses out to graze in the cool afternoon. She was surprised to see that same BMW drive around the block for the third time. She had seen it from the kitchen window about an hour ago. It stuck in her mind because an expensive car like that was not common in the area. Then she remembered the dirty coffee mugs on the kitchen table and the sink filled with last night's mess. They'd go to MacDonald's for dinner tonight.

II

AS-FAULT

CHAPTER 9

The October morning was crisp and clear, giving the promise of a bright energizing day. The calendar says the year begins in January, but to some people, and Marisa Rait was one, the year begins in September. Everyone is back from summer holiday; schools are open, wardrobes refreshed with cuddly sweaters and new shoes. So, Marisa celebrated the New Year in the fall, not with a bash, but with the optimistic outset of a fresh cycle.

This morning she was up before the sun. She nudged Warren softly. "Time to get up."

"Umm," was the muffled reply from under a pillow.

"Warren, come on, it's five-thirty." She whispered.

"Five more minutes." He dug deeper into the blankets.

"Not even one. I'll be ready in fifteen minutes. A shower will wake you up." She shook him again.

"Okay, okay. Damn it. What time did Chez say to meet him?"

"Six-thirty at the entrance gate to Camden Race Track. He and Bobby Oakes, the trainer, will be waiting for us there. If we hurry, we can watch the horses work out."

Warren could not care less about the whole matter of horses, but Chez had invited Marisa so many times that by now it would be rude not to accept. They had agreed to meet this Tuesday morning for breakfast with horse owners, trainers and jockeys at the track cafeteria. It was a world that awoke before dawn and finished its business by the time white-collar workers were contending with the headaches of rush hour traffic.

Warren pushed back the blankets and stumbled toward the shower. The tile floor was cold beneath his bare feet. "Are you sure Chez will be there?" He grumbled.

"Of course, I'm sure. I spoke to him last night. Chez is at the track every morning now with Bobby. I wouldn't be surprised if one day they bought a horse together. Chez is a gambler, but I think he'd like to bet his money on his own horse." Marisa pulled a black turtleneck sweater over her head, and took her old red ski jacket from the back of the closet. She picked up the black walking stick. "I'll meet you in the car." She called over the sound of running water.

Warren drove silently. Next to him, Marisa appeared eager and happy; that pleased Warren, but the shower had not washed away his distaste for this outing. He disliked and distrusted horses and anything to do with them.

Chez and Bobby were waiting in Bobby's old Chevy by the entrance booth when they arrived. Their passage was cleared and Warren followed Bobby to the parking area beside the practice track. It was difficult to discern men from women. Everyone wore heavy jackets, some in cowboy hats, others with wool caps pulled down over their ears. Everyone seemed to know each other and exchanged '*good morning's*' while intent on watching the horses.

"That's the horse going around the inside rail," said Bobby, pointing. "He's the best I'm working with now. I think he's ready to show some real money. Look at these times, Chez." He reached into the pocket of his corduroy pants for a scratch pad. Bobby winked at Marisa and cocked his head toward Chez. "He's my expert now."

"I've told Bobby how you love horses, Marisa. He's never been married, calls the track 'home' and considers the horses he trains his children."

Bobby chuckled uncomfortably. Like Marisa, he was one who didn't discuss his personal life. Their eyes met with understanding. Marisa and the trainer became instant friends.

Bobby smiled. The crinkles around his mouth and hazel eyes, Marisa perceived, were less from age than from smiles. He was anxious to answer her questions so she might have an educated sense of the goings on.

Chez, the Calabrese, put his thumb to three fingers of his right hand and shook them, badgering the trainer. "Eh, Bobby, you know I don't fool around. You think I come down here early every morning because you such a nice guy, eh?" I pick your brain! Marisa and I gonna buy a horse together soon. Eh, Marisa?" He slung an arm around her shoulder showing that they were in cahoots.

It was Marisa's turn to wink, going along with his game. "Sure, we're just waiting to find the right horse. But don't worry, Bobby, you'll train our champion."

Bobby pushed his stopwatch as the Bay horse galloped past the pole. "This is called 'breezing', Marisa, when he exercises alone. It gives us a good idea of the speeds and lengths he's capable of doing but not necessarily how he'll perform in a race. There are many distractions on race day, but that's when you determine the true horse. This fella did forty-nine seconds and change in four furlong yesterday. An excellent workout, huh, Chez? Now I just have to find the right jock for him and wait until post time. I 've entered him in a six-furlong race, a good start."

Chez looked at his watch. It was already nine-thirty and much warmer. The track had to be cleared by eleven. "If I'm going to get off to any start at all, we better get some eggs and hit the road."

Bobby had his field glasses up and didn't take his eyes off the horse. "You guys go ahead.

I'll meet you in the cafeteria. Order me four eggs over light and a small steak."

All the while, Warren had been standing on the sidelines. His mind was on things other than horses and eggs. "Chez, take Marisa to breakfast and drive her home, will you? There's a meeting at the bank; I can't be late." He put his arm around his wife's shoulder and sought her eyes for understanding.

"Thanks for taking me, I'll be fine,'"" She kissed him good-bye and watched as he walked off to his car,

Conveniently, for Marisa, Chez was able to drive the car up to the large cafeteria. The low building resembled a mess hall with long tables covered in blue plaid oilcloth and crowded with hungry people. A rich aroma of melted butter and coffee drifted among the rafters. He helped Marisa to a bench. "Fried or scrambled?"

"Scrambled, Chez, thanks. Dry toast."

"Bacon and potatoes on the side, coming up."

Bobby arrived, hung his sweater on a hook against the wall and sat next to Marisa. "Did you enjoy the workout?"

"Very much."

"Marisa, I've owned and been training horses for twenty-five years. I love horse and the world here at the track. I put owner, horse and jockey together; it's a team and I'm the coach. I'm not a gambler. Chez, with his construction work, he's all business, but here at the track the gambler in him comes out. He likes the game. Chez told me about your accident, Marisa. Maybe this would be a good change for you. You don't have to jump horses to enjoy 'em. You and Chez would make a fine partnership. You might find this mode of horsemanship suits you better than the previous one."

"Heads up, everyone! Marisa, this plate is yours and Bobby is right on time for his." Chez said, setting down the hot platters and sat beside her on the bench.

Bacon and eggs had never tasted less mundane to Marisa. "Are you considering owning a horse, Chez?"

He sipped his coffee and checked Bobby's time charts. "I am, Marisa, but I want a partner to share my enthusiasm and the work - someone who will rely on Bobby's talent. You can't pick that guy's brain. It comes natural to him."

"What do you have in mind? I can't stay home and play cards with the ladies or join my mother's tea parties. I don't have to tell you; Warren wouldn't even approve of a merry-go-round horse."

Chez became serious. "Supposing I put up the cash and you handle the business details. It's a job, Marisa, and to do it right requires time I don't have."

"I'd have a lot to learn."

"We'll learn together. Bobby will teach us what he can. The rest will be our own personal ingredient. The Fasig-Tipton Horse Auction is held here in November. That's next month. It's the best place for us to buy a horse, if we see one we both like. The trainer is the most important consideration and Bobby is the best. What do you say?"

"I say we have a date for an auction. I never thought I'd own a racehorse. I can groom him can't I? Warren can't object to that."

"Baby, you can do everything but ride him and that's only because you're a bit too big for silks." He teased.

She understood the kindness.

They clicked coffee cups. "To a new D'Acarti/Rait partnership."

***

During the next three weeks Marisa went with Warren to look at new building sites for a residential building park. This, he proposed to be more upscale than Raittown, figuring to target affluent customers therefore money wouldn't be so tight. She drove the Corvette while he sat next to her. It was a pleasant time, especially for Warren because she was actively interested in his work. By the time of the Fasig-Tipton Auction Marisa had convinced him that she was capable of driving alone on the highway.

***

On the morning of the sale, Marisa left herself plenty of time to be at the Camden Racetrack for the beginning of the two days of auction. She glanced at her watch - seven-thirty; Bobby and Chez would be there already. The first of the one hundred and eighty horses would be put on the block in an hour. Bobby had promised Chez he would hold front seats for them. With a purposeful air, Marisa drove through the entrance gates of the raceway park into a garden with a mantle of shade trees still ablaze in their scanty autumn dress. The uniformed guard indicated the road to the auction grounds through a tunnel under the exercise track. Within the mile perimeter of the pristine white fencing was pitched a huge blue and white striped tent. There was no wind this morning, yet there was that hard cold that makes coffee from a Styrofoam cup taste almost good and the steady stream of bundled people circulating to-and-fro the vending truck proved it. Marisa was glad of the ski jacket.

A crowd was gathered in front of a long white trailer with gold leaf lettering of Thimberlund Stables. Chez and Bobby were among them. They were watching eight uniformed grooms disembark an equal number of fastidiously curried equines into an area that had been cordoned off with a velvet rope. The horses' manes had been brushed until they resembled hanks of silken thread and their coats shone. It was no wonder this was the Sport of Kings.

"They'll start at a six figure price." Bobby commented. "See that horse?" He pointed to the chestnut being led in a circle. "His sire was the England's leading stud three times. Watch the bidding on this colt."

Chez studied his manual. "That's number #151. Many people are here expressly for that horse. Stallion isn't he?" Chez unbuttoned his cashmere camel-colored trench coat and loosened the white woolen muffler that set off his still suntanned face - the face of a sportsman.

"No one would geld a horse with that kind of blood in him unless either one of them was crazy. You can't put a loco horse on the track no matter who his sire is. A stallion, that's what you want to buy. With a stallion you have a double shot to win, one on the track, the other at stud. Good money at stud."

"Ah, there's Marisa now." Said Chez. "I told you she wouldn't change her mind. Warren was against it, but they have an unusual marriage. They don't try to rule each other's lives."

"Lucky man." Bobby said as Marisa joined them.

After looking at the horses from the many impressively named trailers, they found the seats that Bobby had reserved.

"Good crowd." Chez noted apprehensively.

"Don't be concerned, Chez. Everyone's needs are different. Most of these fellas are in a different category than you. It's your first racehorse. You're not looking to fill a gap in a stable." Bobby was assuring.

The auctioneer and commentator came into the tent and took their places on the platform to the right of the entrance. They were attired in camel hair coats and scarves, in accord with Chez.

The gavel banged. "Bidders take notice," alerted the commentator and proceeded to state the conditions of sale for these horses of racing age. "Each transaction will be televised and recorded for future verification. Hip #1 and #2 have been withdrawn. We open with Hip #3"

Marisa leaned toward Bobby. "What do they call 'Hip'?" She whispered.

"That's a numbered white sticker on the hip of each horse. You'll see."

The auctioneer called, "Bring in your horse. Pretensa, she's out of the good family of Ground Wind. A high-class racehorse, do you want 'er at six thousand?"

"Hip," called out the spotter in the rear of the tent.

"Do you want 'er at seven, seven thousand dollars?"
"Hip"

The auctioneer gargled on in his incredible lingo. "Hip." He upped the price. "Hip. Sold at eighteen thousand dollars." He banged the gavel, and the nervous thoroughbred was led out of the tent.

Marisa looked to see who had bought the filly, but there was no indication among the stone faces. A young curly haired groom led in the next horse, a dark brown two-year old. Without a moment's delay, as if continuing the same sentence, the auctioneer read the dossier of Hip #4. The bidding went quickly and silently. At eleven-thirty, when the first day's sales were over, they had seen seventy horses sold and none of them struck Marisa or Chez in such a way that they wanted to bid. Either the bid opened with an upstart price or the animal was already gelded.

Bobby saw their disappointment. "Hey, tomorrow's another day. Don't start feeling badly now. You haven't even begun to play." The lines in his face bent to form pleasant angles of encouragement. "See you tomorrow." He hurried off to the stables.

On the way home Marisa stopped at the gourmet grocer and bought a tin of caviar, two prime sirloin steaks and Roquefort cheese for salad. She picked up the full-bodied red wine that Warren enjoyed with his steak. To accompany the caviar was the bottle of Ketel I vodka frozen in a block of ice in her freezer.

Warren was welcomed home with a white lace cloth on the dining room table, which was set with their best china and crystal goblets. In the center were a bouquet of roses and a pair of flickering silver candlesticks. In fact, candles were scattered all around, lighting the corners of the living room, the hallway and the kitchen. Marisa was in his arms before he put down his briefcase. She was wearing her floating white caftan; her dark hair cascaded down her back, when she kissed him he breathed her fresh floral scent. Her face was radiant. Sure as there were fleas on a coon dog, he knew she had something to tell him, but he wouldn't ask, she would tell him in due time. It seemed to Warren as a dream, like the nightmare of her accident was over and they were as when first married: two lovers in their own safe space.

After he had showered and changed his clothes, he took the vodka from the ice bucket and sat next to Marisa on the sofa. She fixed him a wedge of toast with a spread of the Beluga, a squeeze of lemon and a dollop of crème fraiche while he filled the iced glasses.

"This is a celebration. You're on the road to new and better things and I'm well and happy." The walking stick was not to be seen.

Marisa rested her head on his shoulder, and in the flickering candlelight, they listened to Billy Holiday sing the blues. Soon the tin was empty and so were their glasses; he went outside to put the steaks on the grill. When he came in and was seated next to her, she poured the wine and languorously told him about the Fasig-Tipton Horse Auction. They ate their dinner. She served coffee and told him that she and Chez were going to buy a horse together. "A racehorse, not for me to ride but to be close to. No more *Leslie Allen*. Just being at the track, watching Bobby, learning about horses is exciting. It's a different phase, like what you're doing is different than Raittown. Neither you nor I will put ourselves in harm's way again. We have a responsibility to be well and strong for each other."

She ran her words together, grateful for the liquor that made speaking easier.

Warren knew that if he argued, it would only create secrets between them. Once Marisa made up her mind there was no deterring her. He looked at her shining, hopeful face and remembered the still white hands he had held in the ICU. He had to respect her passion; she didn't dispute his. Not having to look for happiness is peace; Marisa at peace was safer than Marisa moving from one thing to another in unrest.

It was late when they went upstairs. In bed, Warren reached out to trace the familiar line of her body - the curve of small waist, the beloved arc of neck and shoulder. Warm, nestling. "Ahh, my love." He closed his eyes, and wondered. 'Is anything more selfish than love and sex, an insatiable desire? What is this *love?*' He drew her closer, breathed her warmth. "More than that, it is unconditional giving.' He concluded and sighed.

Marisa was unable to respond. It hurt her knowing Warren interpreted her rejection personally. that it frightened him, made him insecure - his nemesis, but she couldn't help herself. Time had not kept its promise and healed the disgrace of 'rape' nor her guilt of being unfaithful. She wondered how much longer she could deny him and blame it on her injuries.

She was sleeping soundly when phone rang. It startled her. Her hand fumbled for the receiver on the night table. "Hello." She said in fright of what disaster she had been awoken in the middle of the night.

"Marisa, I saw you today. You are still my beautiful Marisa."

That voice - Brad. His voice once had brought the anticipation of pleasure; now it frightened her. The many glimpses of people she thought to be him were fresh in her mind. She slammed down the receiver.

"What is it?" Warren was sitting up, fully alert, waiting to hear what could only be a catastrophe.

"Wrong number." She snuggled next to him, hoping to settle him back to sleep, though her heart was drumming in her ears. Brad had been watching her. Newspapers reported many cases of a thwarted lover stalking his lost love and more often than not it ended in violence.

"That's enough. Tomorrow I'm going to change our number to an unlisted one. We've been getting too many wrong numbers." He fell into a fitful sleep,

Marisa didn't sleep again.

In the morning Marisa met Chez and Bobby under the tent. The auctioneer began the sale precisely at the scheduled time. The first horse was led in. "All right, ladies and gentlemen, let's get underway. This is the final day of the sale. There are a lot of horses, so please have your bids ready." He banged his gavel. "Nobel Prize. This colt is half - brother to a stakes winner of over three hundred thousand dollars. He buffed his shins two months ago, but he's working well and regularly. You can see his workouts in the catalogue. "Ten thousand dollars…"

"Hip."

The bidding continued; the horse was sold at twelve thousand dollars.

An hour later a dapple-gray stallion was brought in.

"Prancing Dawn." Bobby whispered to Chez. "Like him, Marisa? He's got good blood and the horse has picked up three checks already, one a win. You can take 'im out right away. Good times. Great horse for you."

The bidding opened.

"Go ahead, Marisa, bid. Just raise your hand a bit and nod." Bobby urged.

She did half-heartedly.

"Hip." Reported the front spotter. "Do you want 'im for thirty-five hundred?" Asked the auctioneer. "This horse is already in the money."

A man coughed. Marisa looked around the tent to see if she saw Brad in the crowd. It was impossible to distinguish one person from another in their hooded parkas. The chill she felt last night persisted, she was sure he was there somewhere.

"Someone else will bid on this horse." Chez said, thinking she was looking for another bidder."

"Hip."

Marisa watched Chez. He didn't up the bid. Nice horse, she thought but no magic.

"Sold."

Marisa bit her lip and sighed with relief.

The horses were opening at higher prices now.

"Hip #164," called the auctioneer glancing at the clock. It was moving slower than he had programmed. "Bring in your horse, boys." There was a commotion outside. The auctioneer scowled, stood up and looked outside. "Let's get some help here or withdraw your horse. Here he is. Hip #164. This horse is usually off to a good start…"

He was black and glistening as pitch tar, with a deep girth and stood tall and elegant on firm slender legs. The dark horse reared up, allowing his long mane to fall loosely from his neck. He curled up his lips and snapped his teeth shut with the dint of a hard spring trap. His ears were flat to his head. His large eyes blazed. His tail whistled and thrashed about slapping his rump.

"As-Fault is an unusually large horse out of Heavenly Hildy, a stakes-producing mare and sired by Sharp Reward, a high earner in his racing career. As-Fault placed once and showed once. He's got the ability, a good colt with good prospect any way you use him. Do you want him for eleven thousand?"

"That one's got the look of eagles." An observance shouted from the second row.

"Hip." An immediate bid.

Marisa poked Chez. "That's our horse. Shall I bid?"

He nodded.

"Hip called the spotter, acknowledging Marisa's nod.

As-Fault reared again, lather forming on his front flank.

"Take 'im out of here," ordered the commentator.

"Eleven thousand, I have eleven thousand."

Marisa was on tenterhooks. A fat man in the first row brushed his mustache. The auctioneer pointed questioningly to him. The man shook his head.

"Then it's eleven thousand. Eleven thousand?" A breath. "Sold!" The gavel banged in finality.

"He's your horse," exhaled Bobby. "Not my choice. You're looking for trouble with that one. Any problems you bought are your own."

Bobby's bleak attitude didn't lessen Marisa's conviction. "With a name like As-Fault, a personality like fire and a coat that is steaming poured tar, who else should he belong to but Chez and me? Now what do we do?"

"Title passes to the bidder at the fall of the hammer and we, rather you and Chez, assume all risk and responsibility. In that case, I think you better hurry. You have thirty minutes to conclude the sale"

A round bald man appeared and thrust a piece of paper in front of her to sign. She passed it to Chez.

"The Bill of Sale. We're partners, Marisa, we both sign it. As-Fault belongs to us."

They took the receipt to the cashier at the far corner of the tent to make the settlement. Chez had crisp green bills. A stable release was secured and D'Acarti/Rait took official ownership of As-Fault.

Outside the groom was still trying to restrain the maddened horse that was prancing back and forth, kicking his feet into the air, dispersing the crowd.

Bobby, with Marisa next to him in the car, pulled his horse trailer behind the larger transports. His face was screwed up in annoyance. "What the hell are you doing?" He called to the boy. "Bring 'im over here. Chez, take your horse away from that fool. This is just what you don't want a racehorse to do. Damn!"

Marisa was amused. As-Fault was towing the little groom up and about like a steeple-bell ringer. He willingly passed the lead rope to Chez and ran.

Chez tightened the slack on the rope and pulled it sharply. "Ho! Ho!"

Marisa got out of the car with no doubt that strength of mind was more effective than physical strength. "I'll take him." She reached out her hand before Chez could protest.

"Get back, Marisa." Bobby called, pushing people out of his way and running to her side.

As-Fault was arrogant in his superiority; he was bred from a studbook as thick as the Bible for intelligence, speed and stamina. He was tenacious of his right to freedom. He abhorred the confines man imposed upon him, harsh voices and the degradation of spurs and whips, though he would work his heart out if treated properly. All this Marisa read clearly in his eyes and in the movements of his regal body. "Easy, fella. Come on," she crooned opening her hand and offering a cube of sugar. "Come on. Don't be afraid. Come on."

Bobby looked on in wonder. As-Fault stopped balking. He snorted and tossed his head, throwing off a spray of froth. He stamped and pawed at the ground, and then stood completely still, eye to eye with Marisa. It was more than a cessation of movement; it was an allegiance. With one quiver, all traces of tension left the powerful ebony body.

Marisa smiled and nodded. "He's alright," she said, not averting her gaze from those eagle's eyes. Carefully, with her walking stick, she led As-Fault into the trailer. Soon, As-Fault was at ease in a luxurious box-stall that suited his lineage.

It was truly a new beginning, Marisa thought, as she drove home from the track. Strangely, she felt she and As-Fault shared a destiny. It was still early. She wanted to be home well before Warren so she could rest and prepare dinner; so that he would know that having a horse didn't mean she was neglecting him, to show how she honored his generous understanding. She was driving cautiously in the right lane, aware now that she was tired, yet she felt well. She checked her appearance in the rear view mirror to make sure that the elation in her eyes belied her fatigue. But, what was that car coming up behind her? She straightened up in the seat, and looked again. A silver BMW... Brad, coming fast on her bumper. She couldn't swerve; she could only accelerate. He cut in front of her and squeezed her off the road onto the shoulder. The car stopped with a jolt. Marisa's heart was pounding; the sudden surge of blood gave pressure behind her eyes and for a moment she saw only black. She turned off the key, and leaned her head back. Brad parked in front of her, came around and got in her car beside her. He took her keys from the ignition.

"You've been following me." She said with upright astonishment then looked at him squarely. "It's over, Brad. Now, give me my keys."

He reached for her hand. She drew it away quickly. "Marisa, it's not over. I can't stop thinking of you. You changed my life. We had more than fun together, it was a promise."

"You knew I was married, Brad. There was no promise. I'm sorry. I made a mistake. I didn't want to hurt you. I'm going home. Give me my keys."

"I'm not letting you go just because you say it's over. For me it isn't. I love you. I told you that. Do you think I can just forget it? I never said that before to anyone. I won't let you go,"

"My keys." She put out her hand.

"When we were together everything was going well. My work was going well. Sometimes I thought I'd lose it if I stopped the momentum, so I worked harder. It was for you - for us. I knew my life was with you. That's part of love - depending on the other person. You caused that accident at

Hamil Farm. You let your ego put you where you had no right to be." He took a deep breath. "No, I'm wrong, I don't blame you for the accident. I blame Hamil. He seduced you, pushed you beyond your ability. Maybe he had a reason. Maybe you discovered something you weren't supposed to know. I did some checking on him. He gets many of his horses from the racetrack. I also know you write for the paper. You are *Leslie Allen*." He watched her face, but her expression didn't change. She was looking at him coldly. "Remember that afternoon we were supposed to meet? You didn't come. I thought your lesson was late so I went to the barn to surprise you; I would get a chance to watch you ride, but I couldn't find you. You weren't by Scorpio's stall or by your car. The keys were in the door. I opened it and sat inside to wait for you. That's when I saw your portfolio and I read your notes."

"It was you, not Bensen who went through my papers." She said incredulously, remembering the fingerprints on the leather cover of her journal.

"You should be glad."

"Then you sent that grisly package to Mac?"

"What package?"

"Someone sent a bloody decapitated rat wrapped in newspaper with my by-line."

"It wasn't me, but whoever did it, you know what he is capable of. Hamil, you can be sure, wants to get rid of *Leslie Allen.*"

"I don't go near Hamil. He can't hurt me anymore."

"Perhaps he already knows. I promise you, I've told no one. But I don't want to talk of Hamil. It's you and me. You love me, Marisa. When you were in my bed you couldn't deny it. I know how your body arches with yearning. We have the same desire and need. That hasn't changed. I love you."

"How often is lust mistaken for love.?" She glared at him, remarking to herself that desire floats as a bubble above reality. In the face of reality Brad was a lonely man who amounted to nothing more than getting emerging musicians heard, a rented BMW and probably a string of ex-girlfriends. He had no one to love him, to care about or with whom to share a dream - no one that meant anything. He had nothing. She shivered thinking how close she had come to ruining her marriage for this little man.

"Have you no conscience that you've ruined my life? Don't think I'm above destroying whoever keeps you from me."

She looked at him squarely. "That would be me, Brad, only me."

Flashing red lights caught her attention. A State Trooper had stopped behind them and was walking over to the car.

Marisa held out her hand; her stare was threatening. "My keys."

Brad got out of the car, tossed her the keys through the open window, and walked back toward his car.

"Hold it right there." The authoritative voice of the police officer stopped him in his tracks.

Brad sighed, put his hands in his pocket to get his car key.

The officer drew his gun. "Keep your hands on top of your head, and come back this way, slowly, sir."

This is ridiculous, Brad thought, but knew that southern hospitality was off limits on the highway. The cop would just as soon haul him off to the judge and leave his car on the roadside as bat an eye.

"Are you all right, Miss?"

Brad was looking ahead, anything to avoid Marisa's eyes that could be more dangerous than the gun.

Lovely, fragile Marisa with the silky voice she effected so well, Brad knew she could convince the cop, or any man, of anything.

"Yes, Officer, we were at the horse auction in Camden. With all the excitement, I guess I forgot to eat and was feeling dizzy. My friend stopped when he saw me pull over and gave me a Coke. If not for his kindness I would surely have fainted." She picked up the empty can that had been rolling on the car floor since lunch. "I feel better now. Thank you for stopping."

"This yours?" The policeman said, noting Marisa's walking stick.

"Sprained ankle. My friend thought I might have had a problem with the car; that's why he stopped. I'm grateful he did; I just don't know how else I would have gotten help." She spoke in her most disarming Charleston drawl and opened wide eyes of innocence and sincerity.

The officer regarded Brad, who smiled meekly as he stood respectful of his position. He looked once again at Marisa, dropped the gun in his holster and waved Brad on with the back of his hand. "Go ahead."

Brad leaned into the window on the passenger's side of the Corvette and said in a low voice: "See you later. If not, perhaps your husband would like to know about us. I didn't mind sharing you when I believed I had your love but I won't share your love. For me it isn't over, so it can't be over for you. Understand, 'Miss Leslie Allen'?" He went to his car.

Marisa watched him start the engine and merge onto the highway.

The officer said: "Rest until you're sure you're able to drive, M'am. I'll wait with you; there's no stopping on the road here."

She saw that Brad had driven out of sight. "I'm ready to go now, officer, and thank you again." As she drove away her strongest emotion was sorrow. Sorrow for Brad, for herself and for people who cause their own misery.

CHAPTER 10

It was during morning practice. Chez couldn't believe what he was seeing. He passed the binoculars to Bobby Oakes, who focused on As-Fault being ridden by Joey Valcaro at the far end of the racetrack. The young, Puerto Rican jockey was having a hard time holding As-Fault to the rail. The horse pulled on the bit, trying to get it in his teeth. The trainer didn't want As-Fault running madcap, to burn out with the speed. Joey was to hold him back some until the last furlong. It was all right to break from the gate and take the lead, but he must reserve strength in case another horse overtook them.

A brown horse galloped up to As-Fault on the outside. They ran together, nose to nose, with Joey trying to keep restraint. A moment. The brown horse reared, two front feet slashing at the air and the rider was on the ground.

"Runaway." Someone cried, as the crazed horse bolted on the track endangering other horses and riders. Those who saw the incident reined in to avoid being kicked. The riders ahead were unprepared for the chaos as the maddened horse ran through the pack creating a pile-up. Five minutes later the brown horse trotted docilely to the fence.

"You okay, Paco?" Joey asked the downed jockey as the man wiped the freezing mud from his face.

"Sure. I've been off before, plenty. That horse you have is crazy. He bit my horse in the neck. Never seen anything like that before." He plodded off through the sloppy track looking strikingly small now that he was dismounted.

Chez was astonished. "Jesus, Bobby, he tried the same thing in the barn yesterday. A horse was being led past us and As-Fault turned around to bite him."

"We gotta do something." The trainer answered sullenly, sorry he let friendship drag him into an involvement with a horse he disapproved of in the first place. "Otherwise, we'll be banned from the track before we even get 'im out there. I gotta make peace with the other trainer. Let's hope he's a nice guy, and just be grateful it didn't happen during a race. Then the whole thing would have been on film and the stewards would have As-Fault off the track for good. Tell Joey to continue, take 'im around easy. Keep 'im on the rail. He can use the whip on that bastard." Bobby valued his reputation more highly than he did friendship and didn't care who knew it. He pulled up his collar in a gesture of disgust and went off in the direction of the crowd gathered around the wounded brown horse.

Marisa arrived at the stables at eleven o'clock to see As-Fault washed down and cooled off by the hot walker. For twenty minutes, she sat watching the sleek sloped back and full chest parade by on miraculously slim, muscular defined legs. "I'll take him now." She told the groom.

He handed her the lead and Marisa led As-Fault into the barn where it was warm and bright. She used the currycomb on his mane, then the soft body-brush with long soothing strokes until his coat gleamed. He turned his mighty head around to look at her. Had As-Fault been a lap cat, he'd have been purring. For Marisa also, the moments would have been peaceful but that she kept looking about for a glimpse of Brad. The feeling that she was being watched was heavy upon her.

"How'd you do this morning, fella? Where's Chez and Bobby? I thought they'd be here. The race is in two days. Okay, okay, here's your sugar." She pushed his searching muzzle away from her pocket and withdrew two lumps, which he sucked up happily tossing his head. "We'll show them all, won't we?" Marisa pulled the long loose hairs from his mane. As-Fault turned and playfully nipped her sleeve.

"Cut it out!" She swiped him smartly on the nose.

"Nasty habit your horse has, Marisa." Said a glum voice behind her.

"Bobby! He's only playing."

"Some playing. He disrupted practice on the first rain-free day this week and now he's 'just playing' - the disposition of an angel."

146

She patted As-Fault's neck. "What happened on the track?"

"Oh, today? He was great today. Wasn't he, Chez?" The tone was sarcastic. "Really great. Bit Yallame Stable's best entry in the neck, put the kid on 'im in the mud, caused havoc on the track and made me look like a prize ass." Bobby tugged at his collar and began pacing the short distance back and forth in front of As-Fault's stall. "His workouts? Good. Yeah, real good. He can run like hell when he wants to. When HE wants to. Joey couldn't keep him to the rail, no way. You and Chez chose this horse and if he doesn't shape up soon, I'm canning the whole business. I told you he was no good. I'm paid to know horses." He paused. "I don't back loco horses. This horse is something else when you're not here, Marisa. If he's no good, you got yourselves a lot of dog food on the hoof. So, I suggest you be here. It's not my problem." He shrugged to rid himself of the burden. "My problem is the race, day after tomorrow. Make sure that horse sees you. Remember, As-Fault ain't a pet. It's dollars. Lots of 'em."

"Bobby, wait. Please, tell me, will it be all right, with the track officials, I mean?"

The trainer turned back. Some of the fury had left his face. "Yes, Honey, no real trouble. But, I'm telling you straight, that horse waits for you, been that way from the start. Let 'im rest for two hours, then we'll take him over to the small corral and work with him. Other horses will be there, so he can get used to company. You'll be

147

there too and we'll work 'im till he's tired. Some horses are tough to raid, but leave it to Joey to teach 'im. Come on, put As-Fault away and let's get lunch. I'll bring the car around." Bobby was softer than he professed.

Chez came into the barn in time to see Bobby take his leave. "Marisa, I'm going to work. These are your business hours; my shift is over for today." He pretended to ignore the looks of contempt and whispering amongst trainers and owners as he passed down the long aisle toward the door. Marisa was watching him. He turned to wave good-bye, and caught her eye, winked, and raised his index finger and pinky showing the sign of the Italian horns to the bunch chattering like 'wash women'. This gesture was to say: "Screw you Buddy, we'll show you when it counts."

Marisa got the message and grinned; she knew As-Fault would perform; he just wanted to be asked nicely with the respect he deserved.

Lunch at the cafeteria would be trying at best, what with the ill-will As-Fault had created. Marisa and Bobby left the track to find a local luncheonette for their turkey sandwiches. It was two o'clock when they returned. Joey had As-Fault on the exercise track; his bearing separated him from the eight other thoroughbreds working close together at a hand gallop. His ears pricked up as he saw Marisa. His body stretched out in a black stream; in a few strides he gained a full length on the other horses.

148

"He's the best." Breathed Marisa, awed once again by As-Fault's speed and majesty.

"It does look that way. I won't deny you that." Bobby consented, feeling more hopeful. "Here, put the clock on him when he passes the pole over there."

"What race is As-Fault entered in?" Marisa asked

"In a race for horses that haven't yet broken their maiden - haven't won. It's a fast six furlongs."

The laps of hard practice went perfectly; so did the workouts the following day. Bobby, a critical trainer, could neither find complaint with As-Fault's obedience nor doubt his ability. In the eyes of Chez and Marisa and even Bobby Oakes, As-Fault was a strong entry.

It is a rare day during the winter months when the sunshine is warm and people are in airy spirits. Race day was one of those rarities. Marisa was happy even if Warren stood by his conviction and refused to go to the racetrack. Post time for the first race was at twelve-thirty. The Maiden Special Weights was to be the third race. The trainer told Marisa that even if she got there by one o'clock there would be plenty of time to see the horse saddled and led out to the track. However, As-Fault was not time or dollars to Marisa; he was a claim on life. She was in the barn by ten o'clock to meet the track Veterinarian, who was to check As-Fault's temperature and legs for soundness before the race.

Doctor Doyle was resting against the stall, dabbing at his forehead and neck with a white handkerchief when she entered. He was a big man with pale blue eyes and white hair that waved across his head and bristled out from the top of his starched white shirt. Marisa put his age at sixty-five. The fair skin of his moon face was soft and fleshy; one chin sat happily upon the other. He looked to Marisa like a cream puff; for no particular reason, she was wary of the candy coating. The veterinarian was perspiring profusely. He carefully patted his neck with the handkerchief, folded it, patted again and put it in his trousers pocket. In a whisk, pudgy freckled hands produced a clean handkerchief from inside his tatty tweed jacket. He buttoned the jacket and went on dabbing a dark pigmentation now visible at the nape of his neck. When Dr. Doyle walked, he led with his belly, however his upright reputation for dedication to equine welfare preceded even his paunch. He had been at the racetrack for years, in fact, Bobby Oakes told Marisa, he couldn't remember a time when the veterinarian wasn't there. Too often, Doctor Doyle explained, he had seen an animal become the scapegoat for a man's disenchantment with racing. Attempts have been made to get rid of a loser by veiling an injury and putting the horse into a claiming race. It was his job not to let that happen and to prevent the fraud of switching horses in a race.

"Good morning, Doctor. I'm Marisa Rait, Chez D'Acarti's co-owner of As-Fault."

"How do you do, Miss? I guess your horse finds his stall crowded with me in there." He patted his belly, a wide smile forming a perfect crescent.

As-Fault was snorting through a quivering muzzle and stepping uneasily inside the stall.

"Would you take him out and walk him around some for me, please."

As-Fault resisted moving out of the stall, when he did he suddenly sidestepped the vet and tugged on the lead.

Doctor Doyle stood in the center of the barn door. "Fine horse, Miss. He's as sound as can be. Seems to me he wants to win this race. I'll see you at the track before your jockey brings him into the gate. I'll want to check the identification number on his upper lip. I wish you the best of luck with him, Ma'am. Nice to see a pretty lady around here." He smiled, tipping an imaginary hat in an oddly familiar gesture before turning into the barn.

Marisa tapped the hard ground with her walking stick and led As-Fault back to his stall. To her relief, the vet had already disappeared somewhere in the long building. It was obvious that the doctor made her horse uneasy. The less distraction As-Fault had today, the better. Bobby told her that it wasn't unusual for a thoroughbred to work himself into lather before the gates opened.

Half an hour before post time, each trainer would bring his horse to his assigned cubicle in the saddle-up area where they'd meet the jockey. Chez had bought a season box of seats when Camden Racetrack opened. They were never used. They both preferred standing by the gate to watch the horses come up, and be saddled rather than sitting stylishly with binoculars.

Bobby said, "You can learn more about a horse by seeing him up close than reading a six-month old tout sheet that's already history. Somedays horses are downright ornery."

Once Marisa had surveyed the crowd without seeing Brad, she was able to relax. It was beautiful to be at the track and watch the horses and people coming and going, beautiful to see all the pieces come together, and to bet. You had to study the horses and their jockeys, know the trainers and the odds; you had to breathe the air of all this, equate figures, trust your judgement, cross your fingers, put up the money and ride the adrenaline rush.

She didn't bet the first race. Chez collected a measly forty-five dollars on a place ticket and felt optimistic. He was putting all his money on As-Fault in the third. By the second race there were long lines in front of the teller's windows. Almost everyone had his head down, pencil in hand, figuring his bet from the racing sheets. People conferred with one another in hushed tones as they watched the odds change on the television screens that were suspended from the ceiling.

"Some guys never go outside," Chez said. "They watch the board and the race from here where they can jump to the window and place a bet at the right time." He draped a protective arm over Marisa's shoulder. "We'll catch the second race on the tube."

When the windows opened for the third race, Marisa and Chez were on line at the WIN window to place their bets and a conservative bundle for Bobby. The odds on As-Fault were ten-to-one.

Marisa didn't know how As-Fault would react to the explosive shouting when the race started. "Hurry, Chez, will you help me to the gate?" She took his arm.

Bobby was leading As-Fault over the ramp into the paddock as they got there.

Joey rushed from the dressing room. He had finished first on a new mount in the last race and had hurriedly changed to the scarlet and black silks for D'Acarti-Rait. "I'm hot today, Baby." He bragged as he swung into the saddle. "We're gonna win." He set his feet in the irons and tucked his bent knees tightly to As-Fault's flank. "Feels right."

As-Fault's eyes were on Marisa. He stood still. She rubbed his nose and As-Fault, as was his game, sought her pocket. "You're still a baby." She whispered. "After the race. Wreaths and sugar after the race. A deal?" She patted his nose a last time as Joey led him into the small procession circling in front of the track. Doctor Doyle appeared carrying the entrance sheet and certified the identification number tattooed on the upper lip of each horse.

"It is now post time." Came the announcement over the public address system.

For the first time, Marisa was envious of Joey. She wished it could have been she and As-

Fault out there. But that was a silly dream. She watched the jockey canter down to the post standing in the stirrups. He checked his girth and then walked slowly into the gate without any assistance from the old pinto lead pony.

The bell.

"They're off. It's As-Fault taking the lead, #24, Safari, pressing for second place with Trigger Happy in third, coming along the outside. And it's As-Fault at the sixteenth pole.

The crowd was screaming wildly, standing on their wooden seats and pushing against one another to get a better view.

The #5 horse is As-Fault, jockey Joey Valacaro in the red and black silks is sitting back nicely, holding his lead at the half."

Marisa bit her fingertips. She could barely decipher the blurred number on his white saddle blanket.

"Safari is coming along the outside."

Bobby shouted. "Safari's gonna make a move now. Joey sees 'im."

She bit harder on her fingers, daring to watch.

As-Fault shot out of the gate unencumbered into the lead and swept past the post in a blur of black and red.

"As-Fault wins by eight lengths, and he's still driving. A spectacular wire to wire victory."

Marisa was so weakened she couldn't catch her breath.

Bobby was tired from punching vigorously at the air.

"Let's see," calculated Chez, sparkling. "A one hundred, fifty-thousand-dollar purse. Bobby gets ten percent, Joey gets ten percent and Marisa, you and I share eighty percent. That horse paid for himself today." This, he had figured out before the floral wreath was around As-Fault's neck inside the winner's circle.

"Joey," Bobby said aside to his jockey. "He took you for a pleasure ride. You weren't working out there."

Joey leaned down from his saddle. "Easy race for this horse. No heavy breath. He's got speed he hasn't used yet."

Reporters and photographers swarmed about.
Marisa gave As-Fault his promised sugar cube. A gentleman pulled a carnation from the laurel around As-Fault's neck and presented it to her.

Flash! When her eyes adjusted to the light, she saw it was Brad, his fingers lingering on hers as he put the flower in her hand. She withdrew, looked at him scornfully and turned away to find Chez. Last night, in her sleep, she had seen Brad's face looming at her in the fog. She cried out, desperately trying to grab hold of something solid and awoke to find she was in Warren's arms. He was rocking her while her hands clutched at him. It was always Warren who held her and kept her safe, and she unworthy of his unconditional love. The deceitful injustice she had done to him haunted her waking hours as if the nightmare persisted into the sunlight. She dreaded to think that one time he wouldn't be there.

The photographer patted her shoulder. "See you on the front page of the sporting section in tomorrow's paper. Don't often get to see a race like that. Your horse was all by himself out there. He's on his way to becoming The Horse of the Year."

Someone put a bottle of champagne in Marisa's hand. She took a swig and passed it to Chez, who threw back his head and chug-a-lugged. Bobby was leading As-Fault off the track; he called over his shoulder. "Marisa, keep the reporters happy; I'll take him to the barn and cool him off. Doc Doyle has to do a urine, blood and saliva test on every horse after the race. They always have to rule out drugs. Meet us there when you're ready. C'mon Chez."

Marisa looked to see if Brad was nearby, not seeing him, she released Chez's arm.

Joey and Chez eased away from the crowd and caught up to Bobby. The three of them walked As-Fault over the ramp.

Bobby slapped Chez's back amicably. "I owe you an apology. I never expected a race like this. The horse sure has speed and he's got stamina. First time a horse fooled me. Joey just sat there and As-Fault ran his own race. Marisa said he would. Those two are spooky."

"As-Fault represents a lot to her. What's our next race?"

"An Allowance in two weeks. Seven furlongs, not much longer than today's race. He won't have any trouble. He sees competition closing the gap and takes off. I think I'll change my strategy with As-Fault. I'll let him set his own pace. This is one horse not to put blinders on."

A Security Guard had driven Marisa to the barn. She was waiting for them when they arrived. Hearing Bobby's mention of blinders she asked: "Do you suppose something happened to As-Fault before we bought him that caused anger or pain? Perhaps something that surprised him from behind? That may be why he won't let any horse pass him."

"A horse has a better memory than an elephant. They don't forget anything - ever." Bobby said and added brightly. "We'll just rely on As-Fault's memory as part of his training."

Bobby Oakes' natural horse-sense paid off two weeks later with As-Fault's victory of the Ninety Thousand Dollar Allowance Race, followed in ten days by the One Hundred, Thousand Dollar Allowance win. In the next five weeks, Bobby planned to enter the horse in his first stakes race.

Chez was oblivious to the traffic as he drove southward to Charleston. He was formulating plans for the Triple Crown.

***

Brad Novick had supper with the Chief of Artistry Records, who called himself '*The Disco Dynamo.*' They were the same age but Brad doubted if the

Dynamo would see his fortieth birthday because of his ties to the Mafia, who played a key role in bookings, especially of black performers. After dinner they stopped in at the required number of private parties given by the rock warlords. Brad had gotten sucked into the fast lifestyle but believed he was the only one who was truly independent. He'd been to Charleston to see if he could get one of his groups in the Spoleto Arts Festival that spring. For seventeen days, during the last weeks of May and the beginning of June, Charleston is the center of attention of music and art lovers from all over the world. *Light Year*, seen and heard live, would make an impact and create the hype needed to boost their *Galaxy* album up the charts. Brad finished up at two o'clock in the morning with a starry eyed young lady that he took to his bed. He had escorted a stream of girls up the stairs to his apartment at the Willows on the Pond Inn. They required no more coaxing than a murmured endearment. Rarely, did a girl get more than one encore. Tonight's nameless blond reminded him of the tall Nordic girls with hard bodies. This Viking lass had worked her magnificent golden hair into a thick braid that encircled her head like a crown. He lay on the bed, looked up at her nakedness and closed his eyes, locked in his own dream, while she entertained herself with his body.

Brad gave freely of his body but not of his heart. This belonged to Marisa and while soft hands caused his loins to ache for release, his mind sought the joy of reliving the fanciful pleasures he shared with her: the afternoon they took a speedboat to a hidden cove and swam naked playing underwater tag; how they would cook a stew together and sop up the gravy with crispy French bread while sipping Pinot Noir. She had been snatched from his life, leaving a gap he hadn't known existed. Now, gone, alive but not for me, he thought. Wakeful dreams of her invaded the nights, making sleep a provocative promise. She was a presence that hovered close to him whenever he needed her, but could not touch. It was not yet daylight when Brad escorted the blond to her car.

***

"Yes." Marisa snapped as she answered the telephone. It was nine o'clock in the morning and she was luxuriating in bed thinking dreamily about yesterday's race. She sighed with audible relief at Mac's voice. "Sorry, I was rude. We've been getting a lot of telemarketing calls at all hours."

"If you're looking for the picture of you and As-Fault with the winner's wreath in this morning's Chronicle, I edited it out. You with a horse again, Marisa? And with that crafty music promoter handing you a flower? I don't like it."

"The man I met in your office? I didn't see him, but I might not recognize him. It's been a long time." She swung her feet to the side of the bed, sat up, and brightly changed the subject. "Warren's partner and I bought a racehorse. He's doing wondrously well."

"Come to the office, we can have lunch like the old days and you can tell me all about your horse and I'll tell you some astonishing info I dug up about our man, Hamil. How about this afternoon at one?"

"At one." She confirmed.

"There's something more going on Marisa." Mac had a fail-safe nose for a story.

"Nothing more, Mac." She said cheerily.

"Umm, there is." And it stinks.

CHAPTER 11

Marisa woke with a start. The bedroom was illuminated by the diffused yellow glow of the digital clock on Warren's night table. She pulled herself up on one elbow to look over his shoulder at the time - 2:15 a.m., pitch dark and silent in the house. She lay back and tried to get comfortable in the bed, turning on one side then the other. She shivered and drew in the quilt. 'When would this cold spell be over?' The cold had been terrible last week and the forecast was the same for the next five days.

Days were long. Nights were endless, with Warren coming home late, and tired. Marisa usually found herself dozing in front of the television set until eleven o'clock, hearing oppressive news and prompting for energy conservation, while she hugged a woolen shawl close to her body. Loneliness, cursed loneliness. She and Warren were slipping into the old destructive pattern - each so focused and intent on their own goal that the other became mere background. She heard the faint humming of the digital clock. Time was passing, audibly and visually, and most of it we sleep through, she despaired. Marisa didn't want to sleep any longer. The black walking staff was beside the bed. The lighted time read four o'clock, hours and hours before breakfast and the newspaper telling what others in the world were doing. By Warren's deep breathing, she could tell he was sleeping soundly and would do so and languish in bed until noon - tomorrow being Sunday. She got out of bed, dressed soundlessly in the jeans and heavy sweater still lying on the chaise, got into her car and drove off to join the *"Doers"* of the world and As-Fault at Camden Racetrack.

She had left a brief note for Warren on the kitchen table merely telling him where she had gone. There was no logical explanation, nothing that would appease him. It was mean. The only justification she could invent was to tell herself she would be home before he even woke up to find it.

Twenty minutes into the trip, her haughty independence began to fade. Driving on The Expressway in the wee hours of the morning is not easy. I-95 belongs to the Semis at night. The eighteen-wheelers plow through the darkness, pushing it aside. Marisa saw their headlights bearing down. With the velocity of their passing the Corvette swayed. The windshield was bombarded with flying water and pebbles from the giants' wheels. There were long intervals when she didn't see a passenger car at all, and when she did, most were with a sole occupant. Each, she imagined, had a story; some as foolish as heer own.

The guard was hunched over the pot-bellied stove inside his booth clutching a blanket around him. Cold like this was unexpected in Charleston and Southerners were sensitive to it. He passed her through with a weary nod of his gray head. Horse owners are crazy, the old man thought, wishing he were in his bed. Nothing but the only job available for a man his age would prompt him to be there on this freezing Sunday morning.

To Marisa's disappointment, no one was about. The stable stood huge and somber in the moonlight. It was cold but it was clear and she felt better breathing the cutting fresh air than the parched unventilated heat of the past few days. Marisa pushed open the door just enough to squeeze inside and closed it behind her expecting to hear As-Fault's welcoming whinny, but the unlit barn was a quiet dormitory, except for a random hoof striking a wooden wall or the rattle of a tethered chain somewhere in the darkness. She tiptoed down the center aisle, counting as she passed the shadowed noses of horses dozing on their feet inside their stalls. Chez had told her that the electricity was controlled by a master switch but she had no idea where it was or even if she should turn on the lights and cause a commotion because of her own sleeplessness.

Something whirled about her feet and caught on the cuff of her jeans. Rats. Stable rats. She looked down into two pairs of gleaming eyes. Spontaneously, she kicked her foot and stepped backwards, tripping over a bale of hay. Arms and legs thrashing, she slammed agonizingly to the wet concrete floor. In panic, Marisa felt for her cane. It was very dark, such deep silence. Weak tendons

163

and muscles that were not fully recovered had been stretched and radiated pain. There was a sensation of pins and needles as she drew up her knees. She put her hands on the cement in front of her and crawled, probing the hay and shallow puddles in search of the walking stick. Finally, her fingers touched the icy silver of the serpent's head lying against the rough boards of the stall. She leaned her back against the wall and pushing on the stick with all her might, shimmied to her feet. Then, like a blind person, stooped, tapping and poking in front of her, she felt her way to As-Fault's stall. It was empty.

In disbelief, she opened the gate and stood inside. Empty. 'Maybe he was in another stall.' Maybe she had miscounted. She felt numb, her knees rubber. She swallowed hard and brushed the buzzing horseflies from her face. They were all about her, buzzing and batting noisily, in the impenetrable blackness.

Marisa felt her way to the trunk kept in front of As-Fault's stall. There would be a flashlight among the paraphernalia in that locker. Dropping to her knees, she rummaged through the salves, brushes, the hoof pick, the boxes of leg wraps, until her hand closed on the solid roundness of the flashlight. She pulled it out and shone the beam into the stall and gasped. Bloated green flies were diving in and out of the blood soaked straw. There was blood spattered on the wall, large spots of blood trampled into the sawdust.

'As-Fault. As-Fault,' but the words didn't form on her lips. Her head seemed to be floating;

she couldn't feel her feet on the ground and fell in a faint through the buzzing swarm onto the sticky, reddened hay.

A door swung open. Marisa opened her eyes. Still the buzzing. Sunlight jutted in and glistened on the damp floor outside the stall. Whistling. The feed boy. Marisa crawled over to the open gate, found her stick and managed to standup.

"Yee-ow!" Squealed the boy in fright, spilling some oats from his pail as he saw Marisa, bloodied and filthy, emerge from the stall. "Ma'am, you sure scared me."

"Where is As-Fault?"

"He's, he's...over by Doc Doyle."

"Where? What happened?" She demanded not mindful of her condition. "He was fine when I left yesterday. She was trying to control her hysteria.

"I came by early this morning to feed the horse, 'bout four o'clock. As-Fault, he been kickin' his stall and them horrid rats be scurryin' round. I look down and his foot is bleedin'. Well, you know Ma'am, I like that horse. So I took him over to the next barn where I know Doc Doyle is treatin' a horse for the colic. I didn't want them greedy rats chewin' on that leg. Don't worry, Ma'am, it ain't bad as it looks. He ain't bad as you." He smiled. "C'mon, I'll take you - right cross the drive."

As they approached the door she heard As-Fault's whinny. If Marisa could, she would have run to him but she hobbled slowly to where he was tethered, threw her arms around his warm neck and cried. What a relief to cry.

"It's quarter cracks, Ma'am. Don't take on like that. Look here." Doctor Doyle, looking like he had just finished at the haberdasher's instead of working inside a barn, came out of the adjacent stall. "His left front hoof, let me show you. I'm glad you're here. Early for you, though, isn't it, Mrs. Rait?"

She didn't feel she had to explain. Marisa examined As-Fault's raised hoof. It was split and sore like a cracked lip.

"That's quarter cracks, Ma'am. This here, along the coronary band is the horn that's exposed; it supplies nutrition to the hoof. I don't know how he got the injury. Eighty percent of the cases are hereditary, then it does come from pressure too. This horse has been training and working mighty hard. Feel here." He took her hand in his pudgy paw and placed it on the sore leg. "Fever. It's mighty painful, and can lead to infection. A horse's hoof is soft up by the white corona and tends to split." He looked up as a man in a full leather apron entered the barn. "This fellow coming now is my special blacksmith. He's going to screw a patch of mesh screening and fiberglass over the crack to draw it together permanently. Won't hurt him a bit. It will grow down just like the cuticle of your own pretty fingernails, Ma'am." His moist palm fondled her hand. Marisa pulled away. He went on. "I'll put a mild blister here by the band to stimulate circulation and growth. Your horse will be alright, even better if you can get him to a swim farm."

Marisa sniffed and wiped the hair from her face. She was wet and chilled to the bone and her teeth were chattering. "A swim farm?" She was watching the blacksmith gently tend to the hoof. As-Fault's eyes were blank, his abdomen heaving as he concentrated on the sensation in his foot, and tried to understand why, as never before, he was powerless.

"When we finish with this here patch, you take him back to the stall and I'll talk to your trainer about the swim farm. Bobby Oakes, isn't it?"

Marisa nodded.

"He'll explain everything to you. Meanwhile, Ma'am, you look mighty peaked yourself. Go on home. The horse will be fine, just fine." The blacksmith snipped and secured the patch on the injured hoof.

"Will he be able to race? The big stakes is in five weeks." Nervously, As-Fault prodded her back with his nose, pushing her forward against Doctor Doyle's gelatinous paunch that she feared would enfold her.

"No reason why not," mouthed the thick lips close above her. "He'll train in the pool every day, keep his wind up and stretch every muscle in his body." Hooded eyes smiled down with amusement over rolling chins and the oily soiled collar of an otherwise stark white shirt.

She found old Doc Doyle repulsive: the saccharine dime store scent, the perspiration, his soft flesh.

When the blacksmith finished, the vet whistled for the feed boy. "Ned will help you to the other barn, Mrs. Rait. I'll call Bobby Oakes from my office. The sooner we get As-Fault into the pool, the better." He spoke with professional authority. "There's a place not far from here called St. James Equine Therapy. Not many people know about it, but Frank St. James runs a nice operation for 'bout twenty-five horses. I'll see if he's got room. Don't cost much. If As-Fault is there for three or four weeks it will be better than pounding the hard ground here and tearin' out his throat with this cold wind."

Holding Ned's arm she started back to the barn, leading As-Fault.

"See there, Mrs. Rait?" The vet called when she reached the driveway.

"He walks like he's steppin' on eggs. A horse compensates for the pain by altering his gait. See how he shifts his weight. It'll throw him off and he'll get sore someplace else. Don't waste any time getting him the therapy he needs."

Shielding her eyes from the glare of the sun, she squinted at the hulk standing in the dark doorway of the barn. "You'll call Bobby?"

"Sure thing, Ma'am." He touched his hand to his head.

Marisa felt his eyes burning into her back as she entered As-Fault's barn. She was glad to finally be out of Doctor Doyle's sight. "Ned, I'm so tired. I'll hold him. Please clean out his stall for me. It's awful in there."

"Yes, Ma'am," said Ned, and ran to fetch the rake.

Marisa's body ached all over. She rested her head on As-Fault's neck, "A fine pair we are, neither of us can walk very well."

Ned was tossing the bloodied hay into the wheel-barrel. The flies followed.

"What's that, Ned?"

"What, Ma'am, where?"

"Something white, over there, by the corner."" She pointed to the sawdust heaped near the inside gateway.

Ned dug it up and brought it to her. "A tube of skin make-up." She said wiping away the sawdust. "A cosmetic of sorts, maybe stage make-up. Do you know who this might belong to, Ned?"

The black boy looked at the tube, then at Marisa with a bewildered expression. "Never saw that before. It sure ain't mine. Wrong color." He laughed uneasily and wiped a rosy smudge from his fingers. "I's the only one, 'ceptin you, been here. That's f'sure. Ma'am. Ya can see it ain't mine."

Marisa tightened the cover and put the tube in her pocket. She led As-Fault inside the clean stall, gave him an extra sugar cube then closed the gate, and with the aid of her cane, walked slowly to the car. "Thank you again for taking As-Fault to the vet, Ned."

"Ain't nothin'. We just lucky Doc was here. He's a real kind man. Ain't nothin'." He shrugged. His arms hung long at his sides.

It had begun to rain.

Warren was in a rage. He was pacing outside on the verandah when she pulled into the driveway. On the way home she had been pondering the connection of As-Fault's injury and the tube of make-up she found. She had forgotten that her husband would be beside himself with worry and anger.

"Where the hell did you go in the middle of the night? Don't you think of anyone but yourself? Where were you?" His eyelids were twitching.

She climbed the stairs into the house trying to conceal her weariness. "I went to the track to see As-Fault; I couldn't sleep."

"You couldn't sleep? I was there. Why didn't you wake me? What made you so crazy that you had to go off alone? I was frantic."

"Wake you?" They were in the bedroom. She tugged off her boots and was pulling off the wet jeans. "Wake you? Why would I wake you? To ask permission, like a child? You 're gone all day and talk on the phone all night. I can formulate my own life too. I wanted to go, so I went." She exploded, figuring the best strategy was to fight anger with anger, even though she knew what she did was cruel.

Warren seized her bare shoulders. "Damn you, Marisa. I'm your husband. I work hard all day for both of us. When I come home, I'm tired. I expect my wife to understand. I can't satisfy your every whim. You're being selfish."

"That's right, I am selfish. I love you. I want to share a life with you. What is love if not selfish? You've said it yourself."

He bent down and took her in his arms, wanting to express his love physically. It was so long since they had been intimate, since before the accident, before the hospital,

"Warren, you're hurting me. I fell tonight. I'm tired. Let me go."

He carried her to the bed, placed a pillow under her head. His fingers were gentle as he massaged the areas of tension in her back. He caressed her, feeling her body - her entire body, to assure himself she was uninjured. With both hands he cupped her face and tenderly raised it to meet his mouth.

Marisa turned her head to avoid the touch of his lips. She wanted to talk, to tell him what had happened in the barn. She wanted to tell him about Brad, and free herself of the lie that had been making her miserable. Surely her celibacy was making Warren miserable. Her mind was reeling. *'What was that tube of make-up doing in As-Fault's stall?'* She got up and went into the bathroom. She let water run full force into the tub muffling the outside noises, swirling its penetrating warmth around her. The pine-scented bath oil soothed her skin. With her head resting on a folded towel, she watched the steam cloud her image in the mirrored wall in front of her.

At last she relaxed and convinced herself that in the dark of night everything seemed like a nightmare. She was grateful that Doctor Doyle was so concerned about As-Fault. It was still too early to call Chez. She was convinced that they should look at the swim farm together; they should go today. She brushed her foot against the mirror and saw Warren's reflection. The door clicked; he was gone. Reluctantly, she flipped the drain lever and stepped out of the tub. She wrapped herself in a terry bath-sheet. Her mind was rational: What happened in the barn today was significant, the circumstances were all too pat. That make-up could only belong to Doctor Doyle. He must use it to cover that ugly mark on his neck; all the handkerchiefs he used to dab his sweaty skin, those handkerchiefs folded over and over to cover the stains of blotted grease paint. It was Doctor Doyle who had been in As-Fault's stall after she left yesterday. *'Why? Why would he want to harm her horse?* She went into the bedroom to rest on the bed. Warren sat beside her and rubbed her temples. She wasn't alone. She felt better. *'No wonder cats and dogs like their heads patted.'*

"I'm hungry." Said Warren, waking her. "It's late for breakfast but brunch is in order." He started for the door.

"Why don't you ask me what happened? I don't understand you, Warren, I told you I fell last night." She was sitting up against a stack of eyelet pillows.

He stood in the doorway. "I see you weren't hurt. I watched you in the bath. It's never been

172

different - you tell me just what you want me to know. There's no use asking for more."

"You're my husband and you don't even know me. I've made a life for myself now, Warren, and I won't stop living it." She leaned forward on the bed unaware that she was raising her voice. "Why don't you ask me what happened?"

Warren didn't answer. It was infuriating; he never did answer her when they argued.

"Because you don't care, as long as I'm here for you. Is that 'selfish-love' or plain selfish??" She continued adamantly. Unconsciously, she pulled the sheet up over her shoulders not wanting to expose herself. "I'll meet you downstairs at the table. Now, I have to call Chez."

He came back into the room. "That's another thing. You are interfering with my time with Chez. He daydreams of the Kentucky Derby all day. He…"

Marisa brushed her hair that was stubbornly curling in a flyaway fashion. "Your partner is your business. My partner is my business. And my hair is hopeless." Defiantly, she swept it back with a tortoise shell comb. "If you want to know what happened, listen while I call *'my partner,'* Chez."

***

Her name was Anne Bishop. She was an English professor at Charleston College where Chez had been taking night classes. A few after-class dates, a few late-night tutoring lessons and she moved in. Call it love or economics; call it anything - they were happy.   He called her 'Anna.' Anne – 'Anna,' was thirty- two years old, never been married, slim and wore her natural blond hair loose to her shoulders. She was a quiet, young woman, always pleasant, with a nurturing disposition that didn't complicate Chez's zest for life.

For all appearances, Caesare D'Acarti had reinvented himself. He no longer spoke with a double negative; in fact, he'd erased every cliche of a Calabrese immigrant. He always had a flair for fashion and now had the means to indulge his fancies.   Chez worked long hard hours for quality and stood, with pride, behind the work that bore his name. He drove the Jeep that had belonged to Marisa but kept the old cement truck in the garage of his Raittown house as a symbol to always remember where he came from. Thanks to cell phones, he was constantly available to Warren, to Marisa and to Anna, who could pretty well predict where he was: the track early in the morning and with Warren until dark - except Sundays. Sundays they spent together. Chez was protective of his private life.

He was out of bed, fumbling, on the floor for his shoes before Marisa finished her tale. He slapped the still form under the blanket on the fanny.

"Get up."

"Umm." Responded Anna sleepily. She and Chez had been living together since

Thanksgiving; his sudden decisions were now commonplace.

"Get up. We have to go to Camden, something for As-Fault. Up."

Chez met with Frank St. James that afternoon; he'd convinced Marisa to rest at home. He made an affirmative appraisal of the program at the swim farm and in conjunction with Doctor Doyle, arranged to have As-Fault there the following morning. Having balanced the odds of his Triple Crown prospect, the pool was the only chance to put As-Fault back on the track.

Anna was frightened; Chez was a dreamer, his head always in the stars. Her aim was to help him reach those stars. An upset for Chez could change the stability she'd brought into his life and mean the end of her happiness. She wondered what really happened to the horse. Chez had been so vague, he wouldn't answer her questions. Happiness had been so long in coming; please, please, she prayed, don't let anything ruin it.

***

The rain continued all day and into the evening. Marisa was not aware of the weather. Warren had brought her a tray of pancakes he'd made and a glass of warm milk and she slipped into the safe haven of sleep.

When she awoke, she was surprised at how refreshed she was and pleased when Warren suggested they go out for dinner. Mac had recommended a little French restaurant off of King Street that she wanted to try. "Be sure to order the coq au vin." He said. "It's the best in town."

The bistro was as charming as Mac described with polished brass bar rails and flickering gas sconces on paneled walls, candles and flowers on every table. Marisa sat beside Warren on the green velvet banquette in the shadowy corner. It had been weeks since they had had dinner out and they were in no hurry. It was good to be free of interruption - no phone. Warren ordered a bottle of Bordeaux.

They held hands while the waiter poured the wine. Warren raised his glass. "To As-Fault." He begrudged any participation into Marisa's world of horses but her acting out last night pressured the fear that he was losing touch with her. Warren didn't know how to involve himself in anyone's life, even that of his beloved.

They didn't talk much. They listened to the songs of Edith Piaf and other familiar French chanteuse, pretending the happiness that neither of them felt. Warren refilled their glasses, and sat back. As he relaxed, her stress mounted.

Somehow, without being prompted, without any forethought whatsoever, Marisa turned to her husband. Her eyes were bright with tears, her voice was low, her words precise. "I love you. I've done a terrible thing to you and to me, Warren. I never thought I would tell you but I honor you so and …and Warren - I had an affair. It's over." She rushed. "I don't know how it started. I was so alone. I…" Finally, it was out, those words that had been choking her for months. She looked at her husband not knowing what to expect. How could he ever believe in her love, in their life together?

He sat straight, unmoving, her grief reflected in the depths of his dark eyes, within him a bestial rage fought a restraining conscience. Time stood still. His lips turned white. Her words hit him physically, as if he'd been struck by a truck and after the pain of impact the comprehension bled through him so that every part of his body was battered. Her words assaulted his masculinity. What he thought was his, no longer belonged to him. Who he believed himself to be was no more as when he learned he was adopted. Everything in the world he trusted was a lie. His very existence. He wanted to get up. Decency told him to get up, to leave. But he couldn't move.

Marisa felt his fingers clench and open as he released her hand. She had wanted to tell him for so long. She had to go on, she couldn't stop. "It wasn't love. I don't know how it started." She agonized over the words. "Yes, yes, I do. I have to be completely honest. It started because I was lonely - so lonely, Warren. I'd lie next to you at night and feel a wall between us. You, my husband, were only a memory. I'm not blaming you. Believe that; it was both of us. It was easier to go about our business than recognize what we were neglecting. After my accident I thought it was different. I loved that you took care of me and worried about me. I loved that you took time out just so we could be together: shopping, having dinner, and letting our hearts speak to each other. I was happy but that happiness only made me miserable with terrible guilt. When we moved back home from my parents' house it all changed to the old way. You were busy, and I was well and independent. Maybe you thought I didn't need you and maybe I tried to prove I didn't need you. But Warren, I do need you, not in a helpless way but in the way of a man and a woman who are two together as one. And I want you to need me in the same way. But we've been neglectful of each other, unaware what was at risk, and that hurts as much as my guilt and my lies. I had to tell you because I can't live with the lie. Even if it means losing you, I can't live with the lie."

His jaw stiffened and Marisa knew how deeply he had felt her words, deeper than he cared to show. His eyes were dull and cold, filling her with a bottomless sense of loss. He shifted his weight and leaned away from her.

"I met him in Mac's office. He was there on business but was leaving as I came in. When I went outside, he was waiting for me. We spoke. He came to Hamil Farm. We had lunch. I found myself telling him about the horses, the excitement of the Hunt, telling all I wanted to tell you. He listened to me, Warren."

"What is his name?"

She paused. Until now it was an issue she was speaking about. To say his name made him a real person there between them. She remembered Warren's wrath and jealousy before they were married; she didn't want to put Brad in jeopardy. Warren's vindictive nature had no scruples.

"His name?"

Her confession started, she had to continue. "Brad Novick. I told him about you and me, that our lives were no longer connected. He told me what I was doing, jumping the horses, was dangerous, that I didn't have the experience. I paid no attention; I didn't want to hear those words. I was feeling powerful, invincible. We did all sorts of things together: sports, museums, movies. I'm telling you so you'll know everything. Warren, it wasn't love. I was with him because I couldn't be with you. You are all I ever wanted. I want you now. I love you. I was unmindful of the future of faithlessness. I thought I could control it but I forgot that other people are involved and get hurt, not you or me alone, but Brad also. I didn't want it to happen. I wasn't myself. I was possessed by the thrill of the horses and the admiration given me from Brad and Mr. Hamil. Rather than trying to help our predicament I tried to escape, thinking I could go back and it would be the same. But it isn't. Cheating and lying are ugly. I would never let it happen again. I would rather we parted." She lowered her head and her voice dropped to an almost whisper. "I had to tell you." She sat back, frightened that he might get up and walk out, tell her to pack her things, that he never wanted to see her again. She deserved it, but she had given him the honor of truth. She looked up from her hands to Warren's face, the tears streaming down his cheeks. Instinctively she moved forward to wipe them away but discretion was stronger and made her hesitate. A man such as her husband did not permit witness to his vulnerability.

Warren didn't get up. He finished his glass of wine, poured another before the waiter had a chance. He took Marisa's hand and held it. She didn't know what to expect. From his expression she thought he didn't know himself. He raised her hand from her lap to the table and looked at their fingers intertwined. "Like when we were married." He said solemnly, and looked at her steadily before he released her hand, feeling they had no right to touch one another. "I've cheated on you too, Marisa, I denied it to myself for years. I've been on a roller-coaster ride of ups and downs. All day and night my mind was on myself - my business. I loved it passionately. I didn't want to leave it. It was my mistress and Marisa, at night when I'd feel you reach out to me, I'd pretend that I was asleep because I was with my mistress - a demanding, jealous mistress."

Neither spoke.

The waiter stopped by the table, then thinking better, not to interrupt, turned away.

"It's over." He put his arm around her and moved her head to his shoulder protectively.

She had never felt such love. To almost lose and to have another chance is to know the value of life. Warren was her life. Yet she wasn't secure that she could trust his tranquility; this acceptance from a proud possessive man whose wife has just told him that he had been cuckold, puzzled her.

He tipped up her chin.

She tried to smile and succeeded in turning up the corners of her mouth wondering if it is possible to summon credibility after discovering your truth is a lie; maybe it's easier to forget?

The waiter was getting antsy; he came over to the table with his pencil poised on his order pad. "The kitchen will be closing shortly."

"Just the check, please." Warren said.

From the moment Warren opened the door and Marisa stepped inside their house, she felt awkward and self-conscious. Ghosts, whose eyes were upon her, now haunted what had been the home they shared. Warren, too, sensed it. As she had feared, the confessions in the bistro, when faced at home, became a living reality that hadn't been exorcised.

"Would you like some tea?" She asked, procrastinating, not wanting to go upstairs into the bedroom.

"Sure." Warren said stiltedly and sat down on the sofa with the day's paper.

After a few minutes Marisa returned from the kitchen with a tray of cookies and tea, which she set on the table in front of the sofa. She noticed Warren's face had become somber again and he appeared deep in thought, as if during the time it took the water to boil, all that had passed between them in the candlelight of the bistro was brewing in his mind. And now he was holding himself together by the sheer power of will. The atmosphere was strained and tense. She sat in the chair opposite him and poured the tea. He kept his attention to the news. Time dragged. Finally, she put her teacup down and went upstairs.

Marisa did her toilette slowly, tied up her hair with a ribbon and came out of the bathroom wearing her pink satin gown; feeling exposed she reached behind the door for the matching peignoir to cover her bare shoulders. But, Warren was not in the bedroom. Taking a deep breath, she went out into the hall and started down the staircase. She got as far as the newel post on the landing and stopped. Warren took no notice; he had turned off the lamp and sat, unmoving, staring into the darkness. Marisa turned and went back up the stairs. As she reached the landing she heard a loud crash.

Warren had swept his hand across the table in front of him sending the china shattering. In a few giant strides he was at the top of the staircase where Marisa had fortified herself for the anticipated onslaught of his realized fury. Strong hands pinched her shoulders as he yanked her around to face him; his burning eyes looked down at her. He pressed her to his chest and held her tightly. They stood together; it was a fearful moment, each trying to seek affirmation to what he claimed as his own. The strength went out of his arms and he released her gently. He slipped the satin bow from her hair and spread the dark mass around her face. He untied her robe, which slid to the floor. With fingers, gentle as feathers, he traced the length of her arms to her hands and raised them to his lips. "You are my wife. I will protect you always, even from myself. Nothing must come between us and nothing must invade our home."

Marisa took his hand. Together they walked into the bedroom.

"I would like us to have a baby." He said it plainly; it was his greatest desire; it was all he ever asked of her and she had to refuse.

"Not yet, Darling. I'm not ready yet. Soon,"

He made no argument. It was a new beginning of trust.

The irresistible attraction between them was at last rekindled. They made love. For Marisa it was the return to the 'before' time: before John Hamil, before Brad, before she and Warren had let outside life separate them. Warren was truly her husband and the lover that had left her when Raittown was born. It was a tender and giving act that expressed devotion and belonging. It was, thought Warren, a consummation far beyond the vows of marriage. In the morning the ghosts were gone.

CHAPTER 12

Warren freed a few hours so he could take Marisa to the racetrack early Monday morning. The goal was to get As-Fault the best treatment without delay. Unfortunately, Chez had a scheduled groundbreaking for a foundation and had to be there to direct his crew. which had priority on his time.

Doctor Doyle was in the barn when they got there. He smiled the southern gentleman smile when Marisa introduced him to Warren, and explained quarter cracks in layman's terms as he checked the patch on As-Fault's hoof. When he finished his examination, Marisa led her horse outside where Bobby was waiting. She lined the floor of the trailer with a thick cushion of hay before putting As-Fault inside.

"Where's Ned?" She asked the vet. "I didn't see him this morning. I thought he would help us."

"There's a new kid working now. Ned called the employment office earlier, an emergency, someone sick in his family. Ned went home, down to Florida. Don't know if he'll be back. Nice boy."

Ned's sudden disappearance seemed strange. Marisa kept her worries to herself and didn't voice her skepticism. Wanting to adhere to the business at hand without delay, she said brightly, "What time will you meet us at the swim farm, Bobby?"

"Doc and I will be there after practice. You won't have to wait long."

It was an hour's drive to the swim farm. They drove down a road dotted with muddy puddles. Warren didn't need Marisa to tell him to go carefully, not to jostle the trailer and throw As-Fault off balance. The road twisted and ended in a circular clearing where an old trotter's sulky adorned with flowerpots of dead geraniums rested beside a number of horse trailers. Straggly Oak trees drooped their rain-laden branches down so low that the moss brushed against the roof of the car. The white painted shingle house was typical of the county's farmsteads. An empty corral joined the house to a long aluminum Quonset hut with a corrugated metal roof. The plastic insulation nailed to the windows was steamed, making it impossible to see inside. A stack of black trash bags was against the house where water dripped from the drainpipe in a steady plop, plop on the uneven ground.

Warren maneuvered around the maze and stopped in front of a door with a cock-eyed sign, which read - *OFFICE.*

"Let me make sure Mr. St. James is here before you get out in this mess." He made his way around the puddles to the Quonset hut. A minute later he returned to the car, moved it as close as possible to the door, and carried Marisa, over the muddy ground, inside.

The chamber they entered was cold despite an overhead hot air blower. It housed a pool of opaque green water that was about eighty feet long by thirty feet wide with a catwalk jutting three quarters down the length.

"Hello, I'm Frank St. James." Said the long-legged man, who quickly brought over a chair for Marisa. He had a three-day's growth on his face, which had the look of permanence rather than neglect. Tall, and lean, he moved spryly around the slippery perimeter of the pool. Close-set brown eyes darted from Marisa's face to Warren's; he spoke in the same snappy manner in which he moved. "You're Mrs. Rait, Ceasare D'Acarti's partner. I met with him yesterday." He stepped forward, on thick rubber-soled boots, extending his hand to each of them.

"Yes." Said Marisa, pushing back the hood of her slicker and shaking off the rain. "This is my husband, Warren." The echo of running water circulating loudly in the pool area made it necessary to shout. "Our horse is outside in the trailer."

"Doc Doyle called and told me you were coming. Never did business with that vet before. Got a flat racer with quarter cracks, huh? Too bad, but we have success fixing them - three to four weeks. He told you that?"

Marisa nodded.

Frank inhaled deeply and continued. "You folks ever been to a swim farm before?"

"No. No we haven't." Warren called over the racket. "It was nice of you to take the time to show Mr. D'Acarti around yesterday. I hope we didn't disturb your Sunday."

"Nope. I work every day. Let's take a look at your horse." He put two fingers in his mouth and whistled. A trick Marisa never mastered and always envied. "Hey, Jimbo." He called loudly. "Give me a hand unloading that trailer outside. Be back in a minute, folks." He turned to the door, stopped and reddened. "Oh," he said, grinning like a schoolboy who had forgotten his manners. "Want some coffee? It's on the shelf over there. Help yourselves." He slapped his hands on his thighs in finality. "I'll go out and see to Jimbo. Help yourselves." Another slap and he was gone.

Warren shivered. "Doesn't exactly give you an incentive to swim. I hope this will help As-Fault."

"The vet says it will and Bobby agrees; Frank St. James is optimistic. What else can we do?" She said looking at him steadily, consciously including him. She stood and slipped her arm through his. "They even have a tread-mill for the horses here. I wouldn't have imagined such a thing."

As-Fault's whinny announced Jimbo's arrival. A lanky boy of about eighteen came down the skid proof canvas aisle leading the black stallion - his head high, imperious even in his pain. Frank followed behind.

"Now let's take a look at those feet. Strange thing, quarter cracks, they're easy to cure but if it's a hereditary condition they come back one place after another till all you can do is retire the horse. Any history of quarter-cracks in his papers?" He was squatting down lifting and tenderly examining each of As-Fault's hooves.

"What do you mean - retire?" She didn't like the finality of the word.

"Take him off the track; use him for hack, or show, you might even hunt him, but the steady abuse of training and the race itself is what will destroy the feet if he's got the tendency. Anything in his papers?"

"Nothing." She reiterated Chez's words of assurance to her. "Doctor Doyle explained the problem to us. There is no indication of quarter cracks in As-Fault's history."

The telephone rang. Frank looked over to the makeshift desk in the far corner. "Excuse me." He sprang to his feet to answer it. When he came back he appeared annoyed. "That was Doctor Doyle. They'll be late. We'll have to put off swimming your horse until they come. I won't do anything without the vet's prescription. It'll be at least an hour and a half until they get here. What would you like to do?"

Warren looked at his watch. "Marisa, I'll take you for lunch, if they're not here when we get back we'll have to leave. I must be in the office. I'm sorry but we have a closing this afternoon." He hesitated.

"I won't leave him. We'll go for lunch, by then Bobby will be here. I'm sure he'll drive me home."

After a brief lunch, Warren brought Marisa back to the Equine Therapy Swim Farm, and saw Frank make her comfortable in the tight Victorian parlor of the house. He looked at her with trepidation, not wanting to leave and unable to remain.

"Don't worry. Bobby will be here in a moment. Go ahead, Darling. I'm fine. Really." They heard a car in the driveway. "That's probably him now."

Warren went outside to speak to Bobby while Marisa pulled herself out of the low couch and went to the window. She saw her husband speaking with the trainer. When he came back inside he looked consoled. He took her hands. "He'll take you home when you're finished."

"I won't be late. Now go ahead."

"You're okay with that?"

"Yes, Darling, and thank you." She kissed him before he left, then watched the car go out the driveway. Looking about the room, she was heartened by the many photographs of Frank shaking hands with trainers beside laurel-laden horses; some names she recognized from the track.

Jimbo came in from the barn. "We're ready. Let me help you, Mrs. Rait."

She declined his offer politely.

"Well then, I'll meet you over there."

The rain had stopped. Using her walking stick, Marisa plodded her way through the mud. Nearing the metal building, she heard shouts and hooves stamping on concrete – shrill bellows accompanying chaos, which it was. Blindfolded and tethered, As-Fault was as crazed as an animal caught inside a flaming barn.

"What are you doing to him? Stop!"

Jimbo was holding the lead while Bobby was pulling As-Fault by the halter, trying to keep him from rearing. "Marisa, help us." It was a plea.

"What are you doing? Leave him alone. He'll hurt himself slamming down on his feet. Stop." She made her way toward the pool, grabbed the lead strap from Jimbo, pushed Bobby aside and pulled off the blindfold.

The four men appeared helpless as they watched Marisa soothe and eventually gain control of the frightened horse.

"My God, if the cure is going to get him killed, let's forget it right now." She shouted.

The sweet acrid odor identifying the presence of Doctor Doyle permeated the humid air in the metal room.

The vet stepped from behind Bobby. His starched collar had wilted. He touched his hand to his head. So controlled, so congenial, his bulk seeming to melt into the mist. "It's good to see you here, Marisa."

Frank was by her side in two strides. "Mrs. Rait, I'm so sorry. Never seen a horse react this way. Procedure is we blindfold them the first time if they're afraid. Your trainer tells me you can get

190

this horse to do anything. Once he's in the water he'll like it. Swimming comes natural to horses. They do what you call the doggie paddle, but it's the same gait they as a trot, only you can control the amount of effort or how fast they tread water by how quickly you lead them. The slower you go, the faster he must propel his feet to stay afloat. Here, let me show you how to do it, then maybe you can lead him down the ramp. There's a relaxing whirlpool at the bottom. The swirling action promotes circulation. He'll be able to stand there; the water's only five feet deep. You lead him around just as you ordinarily do, only we use a pole instead of a slack lead rope."

Frank's explanation eased her fears. "I can do it." She leaned her walking stick against the wall.

"The pole is heavy." Frank warned.

"He'll do better with me." Marisa, speaking gently, and following Frank's instructions, hooked a leather lead to the right side of the halter. Jimbo handed her a long rigid pole with a six-foot chain, which she connected to the other side of the halter. She was to carry the pole along the perimeter of the pool. Jimbo would assist her from the catwalk by guiding the lead.

Frank was next to her. "Good, Mrs. Rait …'Marisa'... if I may? When you carry the pole, you're the navigator. Can you manage?"

"Yes."

"It's easier if I take some of the weight." He took the end of the pole. "Walk forward. That's it. Stop when he reaches the end of the ramp. We'll

191

give him the benefit of the whirlpool for ten minutes."

Jimbo had taken his position on the catwalk.

"Think of this as a spa for horses. They take to the baths like you would enjoy Palm Springs."

As-Fault appeared completely composed, snorting through flared nostrils. He proceeded to the end of the ramp without hesitation, much to Frank and Jimbo's amazement.

After ten minutes Frank said. "Alright, Marisa, walk him around the corner of the pool. That's deep water, eight feet, here's where he'll start to swim. Fifteen minutes will be enough the first time."

Marisa had been convalescing from her accident for six months and had been careful not to do any strenuous exercise. Walking without her stick and carrying the heavy pole were exhausting. Her arms ached. She turned the corner. Jimbo reached the end of the jetty and helped guide the horse into the deep water and wider part of the pool.

"Let him set his own pace." Said Frank, still supporting the end of the pole. "That horse is a fine swimmer."

The trainer and the veterinarian were conferring quietly together. "The swim farm is the right idea for As-Fault; three weeks, maybe four, he'll be back on the racetrack." They agreed.

Frank continued walking next to Marisa. As-Fault, harrumphing through bared teeth, moved his rump up and down.

"See that action? Swimming gives a horse a chance to develop all his muscles, even those not used when he runs."

The telephone rang. "Could one of you get that for me?" Called Frank. His voice echoed.

Doctor Doyle answered. "It's your wife, Frank. Says there's a fellow stuck in the driveway with a trailer; he's up by the road and needs help."

"Blast! Tell her I'll take the car and get him out. Come with me, Bobby; two of us will get it done faster. Marisa, just keep doing what you're doing. Go back and forth and don't worry, Jimbo is here. We'll be right back." He muttered a string of curses under his breath, jumped across the corner of the pool and was out the door, with Bobby behind him.

The closing of the heavy door punctuated their exit. Marisa was sweating from exertion. She didn't realize how much of the weight Frank had carried. She wished Chez were here. From the side of the pool, she watched As-Fault's hooves, and the force of his body boiling the water. Without warning she was overcome by dread. It mounted until it became a tangible pain in her chest. She was struggling for breath, but the deeper she inhaled the more putrid the air became.

She remembered her lunch with Mac; they were in his office and had sent out for a pizza. He was telling her about Doctor Doyle. *"Old Doc, folksy* and *so kind,* helped John Hamil when he first came to America, when he was an exercise boy at the racetrack. Old Doc...Doctor Doyle." Those were Mac's words, now she remembered, he had said, "Sometimes, after Hamil rode a horse, it would develop an injury. Doc Doyle would advise the owner rather than 'put the horse down' to sell him at a cheap price for hack. Hamil gets many of his horses off the track."

'Doctor Doyle and John Hamil.' The apocalypse came to her in a lucid flash. Doctor Doyle arranges the injury of valuable racehorses so Hamil can buy them at a low cost, train them and sell them for a lot of money.

The veterinarian was sitting at the desk, his hand still on the telephone, smiling. *'Good Ol' Doc.'*

Jimbo was on the catwalk intent on As-Fault.

Marisa's mind was whirling. As-Fault was a stallion. *'Greater value as a stallion.'* Hamil wanted As-Fault. Her arms fell to her sides and her knees gave way. She reached out to nothingness and fell into the turbulence.

The water closed over her, locking her into a world that escaped gravity, with neither up nor down. She was spun around and around, bumped and scraped against the grating sides of the pool, all the while being sucked closer to the churning razor-edged hooves. She could see them cutting through the pea soup, catching in her hair and pulling her to the blades of death.

'As-Fault, As-Fault.'

Jimbo didn't see her fall. The splash startled him; he shouted to Doctor Doyle. Nothing could be seen beneath the surface of the water. He dare-not dive in and get caught by the powerful hooves. In disbelief he saw the black horse stop moving. The water calmed and the horse disappeared beneath the slime; the weight of his body carried him straight to the bottom.

In her dream, Marisa felt the silken threads of As-Fault's mane slide across her face; reflexes made her clench the softness in her fists. When As-Fault's feet touched the solid floor of the pool, he contracted his body as if to jump, and came to the surface carrying Marisa with him.

Jimbo easily reached down and dragged her from his neck, out of the pool.

He carried her from the jetty and laid her on the wet concrete floor. Quickly, he stretched her arms over her head and pumped the water from her lungs. At last, she coughed and sat up.

Marisa looked at the faces staring down at her. Frank and Bobby had returned. As-Fault was out of the pool.

Doctor Doyle sauntered over to her, fatherly concern on his face. His thick lips parted and words came out as from an open furnace.

"Are you alright, Miss?"

She knew what he meant. It was a threat, or was she going crazy? 'No. No. As surely as he got rid of the feed boy, Ned, he meant for As-Fault to kill me. Oh, God, this is madness.'

"You're cold, let me cover you." Doctor Doyle took off his jacket put it over her shoulders. A tube of grease paint, just like the one Ned had found in the stall at the racetrack, fell out of the pocket onto the floor. She reached to get it before it was seen but her hand was quickly covered by the vet's hot palm. He unscrewed her fingers from the tube and dropped it into his deep trouser pocket.

Marisa recoiled. His image swayed. With one hand she covered her mouth, afraid she would be sick, with the other, she pushed him away.

Jimbo and Bobby helped her to a chair.

The big man loomed over her, regarded her professionally. "Let her get dry and rest. No harm done." He patted the evidence in his pocket.

That foul smile - it made her skin crawl. It was everything a smile shouldn't be.

Frank brought a clean horse blanket and wrapped it around her back. "I'll help you to the house. My wife is there. She'll make you comfortable. We'll take care of your horse."

Marisa lay chattering under a flowered quilt on the sofa in Mrs. St. James' parlor. The radiator clanked. Mrs. St. James tiptoed into the room; a fresh-faced young woman, blond bobbed hair and an athletic body emphasized by black tights and spiked platform shoes; a loose gray sweater slid over one shoulder. She moved around the cramped quarters with measured little steps, adjusting the crocheted doilies on the chair arms and tabletops. Her persona so contradicted her environment that it added to Marisa's unworldly state of mind. Marisa sat forward. "May I please use your telephone? I want to call my husband to pick me up."

"Of course." Mrs. St. James said cheerily. "But your trainer and Doctor Doyle seem to insist on taking you home. Or, Frank will drive you, if you like. We're all glad you weren't hurt. Terrible thing, falling into that water; never happened before. Have some tea. It will take away the chill."

Marisa was grateful for the soothing drink. It did stop her from shivering. "Thank you." She said draining the cup. She heard approaching footsteps outside and pulled the quilt tighter around her bare shoulders as Frank and Bobby came in. "Where's As-Fault?"

"He's been dried and rubbed with a poultice for stimulation. Frank pin-fired his legs to create better circulation and put the wrappings on. He's blanketed in a warm stall in the barn having some oats. It's you we're all worried about. Your clothes are dry now." Bobby handed her the sweater and jeans, still warm from the dryer, along with her cane. "I'll take you home."

***

While the three-week treatment at St. James Farm was a period of anxious waiting, Marisa's optimism was rewarded with a rippling muscled horse, fit, and eager to run. As-Fault shook his head up and down, danced sideways and stamped his feet in impatience. At his first workout on the track, the stopwatch confirmed that his speed was up; his stamina seemed endless. Marisa would not go near

Doctor Doyle. Chez spoke to him and relayed the outcome of As-Fault's examination to her.

"The vet says our horse is sound from head to toe. The quarter crack has healed." He paused, put his hand to his chin and regarded her critically. "Marisa, do you have hard feelings toward Doyle, something personal? It's rude the way you avoid him. He recommended the swim farm in the first place. You should thank him that As-Fault is able to run."

"Don't worry, the doctor and I understand each other. We get along just fine."

"You've been acting strangely since your famous swim. Did you drink too much of that green water? Don't forget, Doctor Doyle is the official track veterinarian; he's important to our position here." He tapped his forehead with his index finger. "Think, eh?"

It was the first time she had seen Chez irritated. "I'm sorry. He just repulses me. I guess I let it show."

***

On race day, though As-Fault was not one of the favorites, those knowledgeable of his workouts considered him an excellent bet. The 5:1 odds made the #6 horse, As-Fault, a very interesting shot, indeed, for this high stakes event. When the windows closed there was a great deal of money riding on the horse.

"It is now post time." Came the nasal announcement from the loudspeaker.

Marisa was pressed to the rail.

"And they're off. Number six takes the lead, setting a fast pace. Number nine is second, number twenty-two and number four on the inside."

Marisa, on tiptoes, peered over the head of the man next to her to see the eight horses round the bend. Among the exuberant crowd, one pair of eyes faced her direction. Doctor Doyle's eyes met and stared into hers. She tightened her grip on the serpent head of her walking stick and forced herself to look away. The horses were heading for the finish. As-Fault was in front. He crossed the wire alone, far ahead of the others.

Joey dismounted immediately and walked As-Fault into the winner's circle. Only Marisa noticed the irregular gait and the bloody trail left behind. The man to her left excused himself and moved away from the fence. Marisa looked across the space and again into the cold visage of Doctor Doyle. He smiled. Hideous. She rushed past him on the way to the paddock.

Once more, As-Fault was scheduled for equine therapy at the swim farm, but this time the prospective was not favorable. The vet told Chez that another race could cause severe damage, "Enough to put the horse down; it would be a good idea to sell him for hack."

With sadness, Marisa regarded As-Fault as she had envisioned herself after her accident: a vital machine made immobile and ineffectual. She wouldn't let it happen. She had identified her Evil; it had a name - John Hamil. She would fight him. Hamil wanted As-Fault; he would get him. As-Fault was not at all ineffectual.

CHAPTER 13

Ellen Coleman's kitchen sink was grubby from yesterday's family assault. She and Marisa sat facing each other across the table, separated by motive and a variety of perceptions. For over an hour Marisa had been listening to Ellen's plans for the Rotary Club's Citation Breakfast where her husband, Larry, would be given the award for 'Rotarian of the Year.' Each year the Rotary Woman give the award to a member in recognition of their outstanding work for the community. Ellen, too, was honored having been appointed Chairman. Already she was busy planning the seating arrangement and flowers for the August event.

Marisa endured her discourse, looking for an opportunity to interrupt. "You make the best coffee, Ellen." She smiled pleasantly having accepted a second cup and knowing Ellen's hunger for compliments.

Ellen shrugged. "Thanks. Oh, I meant to ask you, how's your horse doing at the track?"

Marisa lowered her eyes. "We've retired him. Quarter cracks. I don't know what to do. He's not valuable at stud anymore because they say the condition is genetic. No one will breed a horse with a possible hereditary problem, even though he has speed and conformation." She waited and watched Ellen's face soften with sympathy.

"I guess you're right. What will you do with him?"

Marisa sipped the coffee, sighed wistfully and took the first step. "Ellen, do you still have an empty stall in your barn?"

Ellen nodded.

"I'd pay you to keep him here. I'll come every day to groom him and walk him. You could ride him, if you like, even train him and show him. He'd be a strong entry." She said with enthusiasm.

Ellen was quiet.

Marisa remembered how envious Ellen had been when she first saw As-Fault one morning at the racetrack saying: 'To take a ribbon on that horse would turn everybody's head.' Marisa let her toy with the bait.

"If I were to show him, I'd have Mr. Hamil get him ready with me. I know how you feel about him, but I couldn't do it myself; I'd want As-Fault to be a winner."

"Ellen, As-Fault is a winner. He's won every time he's been out. He'll win for you, for us."

"I know how well you said he works for you."

"It's more than that. I love As-Fault. I can't go back to nothingness again. Horseracing isn't my sport. It'll be like old times, only you'll be the rider. I'll take care of him and the stall. You'll earn extra money and there will be no work for you."

"Whatever you pay me, Marisa, I'd use for the training costs. Otherwise, I'd never take money from you." She apologized.

"I want you to be comfortable, Ellen. Board and training is more than fair. Whatever the cost, I'm grateful. As-Fault deserves to be a champion; he has the heart, mind and the body. But you must give me your word not to tell Hamil that As-Fault belongs to me. He really hurt me by not seeing me after the accident. I'm not as forgiving as you are. I don't want to thank that man for anything."

Ellen looked up searchingly. "You don't blame him for your accident, do you?"

"Of course not. It's as you say. No one makes us do anything; we have choices. You can tell Hamil, and anyone else who asks, that As-Fault is your horse; Larry brought him home as a surprise; he belonged to a friend of his." She reached across the table and took Ellen's hand. "Will you do it?" She asked not exactly sure how she would arrange it with Chez. As-Fault belonged to them in partnership.

Her eyes sparkled. "When will you bring him?"

Marisa let her breath out inaudibly. "As soon as he's finished with the treatment at the swim farm he'll be strong and ready to work. I figure three more weeks. I want him well healed and strong, with no chance of a recurring injury."" She put the mugs in the sink. "Let's go out to the barn. I want to make sure I have everything we need. But Ellen, no one can know As-Fault belongs to me. Promise?

"I promise." Ellen replied. *'Marisa was so adamant on secrecy.'* Her head was filled with images of the horse show at Hamil Farm and winning a blue ribbon with the most enviable horse - As-Fault.

***

Chez took his checkbook from a Fendi attaché case and, with a decisive flourish, paid Frank St. James in full for As-Fault's board and therapy at the swim farm. Marisa could see he was already submersed in another role. Rugged boots laced over Levis, a denim shirt and work gloves tucked under his belt. This was the Chez she knew best; this was Chez doing what he did best – construction.

When Frank went outside to put As-Fault in the trailer, Chez turned to Marisa. "This horse has more than paid for himself and his expenses. I'm finished with horseracing. I'm putting my money in a secure investment – myself. As-Fault is yours unless, of course, you want to sell him. Doctor Doyle has a generous offer from a colleague of his". He flashed his most engaging smile.

"Oh no Chez, no." She hugged him around the neck and nearly cried with relief. All the foxiness she imagined she would use …As-Fault belonged to her.

"Take the trailer. Do you know a place to board him?

"I'll bring him to my friend, Ellen Coleman's house. She has a barn with an empty stall."

***

The first chartreuse points of crocus leaves were pushing their way out of the wet ground along the fence of Ellen's corral. Early Spring, Show Season was about to begin and As-Fault, after his training with John Hamil, would be ready to participate in the most prestigious events.

As-Fault had not been ridden in six weeks but made no protest when Marisa put her Forward-seat Jumping Saddle, the one she had used with Scorpio, on the sleek black back and secured the girth. He sought his morning lump of sugar and happily walked with her around the corral.   Then, she handed the reins to Ellen, who did the same.

Marisa knew Ellen was afraid. As-Fault was headstrong and had never been ridden with the subtle control and etiquette required by the English school of equitation. Nor, had a girl ridden him. His tender mouth was accustomed to the deft hand of an experienced featherweight jockey but the firm, yet gentle hand of a woman might be more suiting to his temperament. Presented with a challenge, As-Fault would prevail, as long as he had no conflict. Harmony is long in coming to a horse and rider. In time he would learn, giving way to neither whip nor spur but to integrity and wisdom equal to his own.

"Mount-up, Ellen. I'll hold him." She patted As-Fault's neck and murmured something Ellen couldn't hear.

Ellen hoisted herself into the saddle and adjusted the stirrups. "Feels good. I'll trot him around, then canter."

Marisa stood by the rail watching Ellen take As-Fault through the gaits. Though meek in spirit, Ellen had polished equestrian skills.

As-Fault pulled on the bit when they started cantering. Practiced as a racehorse to run for all his might, he was not prepared for the doling out of his power, the precision timing of restraint and surge which is the initial training for a Jumper. With Ellen's patience and Marisa's words, he learned the different manner he was expected to run. Soon, As-Fault was doing the exercises with the behavior and carriage of a schooled horse under saddle.

When they were finished Marisa helped Ellen dismount. "How was it?"

"Not at all what I expected. I thought he'd try to run away with me. I didn't have to use a crop for the figure-eights. As-Fault has already learned the foot commands; just a little pressure and if I lean hard into it, he changes leads."

"It's funny how love effects humans and animals the same way. They want to please."

"Nobody will surpass this horse after Mr. Hamil trains him. He'll win his class in the show easily. Did you know Hamil is having a big show at his place in August?" Ellen was walking the horse in small circles to cool him off while Marisa sat on the fence. "Has he had any Steeplechase training? Has As-Fault ever done any jumping?"

Marisa ignored the question. "I didn't know about Hamil's show; well…it's in keeping with his personality." She replied, pleased. It was as she expected.

"He's getting entrants from all over the East Coast. It's the first event of the season for national points."

"Have you spoken to him about As-Fault?"

"Only that I have a new horse I want him to train. He sounded less than interested, but told me to bring him over whenever I'm ready. I have an appointment for Monday afternoon." They were walking side by side. "Marisa, you didn't tell me, has As-Fault jumped?"

"We'll let Hamil train him."

***

John Hamil was tired. He carried his after dinner coffee into the dark living room and set it on the table by his wing chair. His eyes fell on the black leather-bound schedule book lying open on the table. It was dusty and open back to June when the lessons abruptly began to fall short of what was required to meet his expenses. The pages were empty. He could only attribute it to the *Leslie Allen* article in the Charleston Post. Margaret had left the paper open on the table in the kitchen where he couldn't miss it. Of course, he was enraged, as Margaret knew he would be. His immediate thought was that it was Marisa Rait's doing, but she had been in the hospital and the *Leslie Allen* column remained in the paper week after week. Certainly it was written or told by someone who had spent time at the farm. He considered Ellen Coleman. No, she was not of the ilk to be so bold. no need to write Ellen's name in the lesson book. She still came along with about ten other sycophants. Actually, he had been waiting for her call. It finally came yesterday; she called to make an appointment - training for a new horse she had bought. He laughed when he remembered her saying it was an extraordinary horse that had hindquarters with the drive of a piston. He had never thought she was capable of such moving expression. She always was a guileless girl, stammering like she was the one tripping over foreign words. As if she would buy a horse from anyone but him? Dr. Doyle took care of that horse at the track. Quarter cracks are easy for a vet to impose. The horse belonged to the Rait girl. After he was 'injured' she boarded him with Ellen Coleman; it was only a matter of time before As-Fault was brought to him.

He walked through the familiar room and switched on the television set, wondering briefly where Margaret had taken the tea service. He hadn't seen it since he'd put the television in its place on the mahogany credenza. That was when he returned from Belgium, about five months ago. Even in the blue electronic glow he could see that the room was no longer tidy and had the stale odor of disuse A layer of dust covered the furniture. He'd have to speak to Margaret about that again. He settled into his chair, closed his eyes for a moment then reached underneath the cushion and withdrew a pink plastic case. He opened it and took out the blond-haired doll. Her name had been Barbie but he and Rose-Marie decided to call her *Rosie*. It suited her. So now he held Rosie on his lap, it was all he had of his daughter. He straightened her miniature riding Habit and began to arrange the nylon strands of hair with a miniature comb. He closed his eyes again remembering how, on the tour, he had brushed Rose-Marie's hair while she sat on his lap and fussed with the doll. After he would tuck her in bed.

Margaret had taken everything of Rose-Marie's into the freshly kept bedroom and wouldn't let him in. It was her eyes that kept him out. Margret hated that doll because he had given it to Rose-Marie, and though she had found its hiding place she dare-not throw it out. He clicked the remote from one channel to another, finally deciding on a movie. It was a chase sequence; they're all the same, he thought. The movies were all the same: violence, blood and satisfaction. Not his satisfaction. Not his getting back at the world for all that had been taken from him: the position on the Belgium Equestrian Team that surely would have led to an Olympic Championship title. being Master of the Hunt, his daughter. He dropped the doll in the case and shoved it under the chair. Now, according to Doctor Doyle, Marisa Rait threatened him again. He couldn't risk a lawsuit: her testimony of his conspiracy with the vet meddling with her horse that caused him to be retired from the track plus the questionable truckload of horses. He would be financially investigated and have the insurance companies and the racetrack on his back. And still were the repercussions of the damned article. Who could have written it? Perhaps it was his own wife; she had been acting like another person, not seeing to his comforts, since he came home from Europe. His mind attached again on Marisa Rait. He gripped the arms of his chair, leaned his head back and closed his eyes. Quite naturally he came upon the only solution. He would ride her black horse. He would be recognized a *champion.* He'd use As-Fault to combat Marisa Rait.

John Hamil turned off the television set. His blood was pounding and he could feel the pulse throbbing at in his temples. He put his hand in his pants, held himself and groaned. No. He wouldn't do it himself tonight. He needed a woman. He'd wake Margaret. She probably had gone to bed. She always escaped into sleep to avoid his advances. He was on to that farce and cursed the physical drives, which enslaved him.

***

Long peels of green paint curled downward from the ceiling of the barn, most of the stalls were vacant; there was a general lack of activity. Doctor

Doyle, his massive frame buttressed by the wide open door, puffed idly on his pipe blowing spirals of smoke into the air. With what seemed great effort, he poked at the bowl and sucked sporadically until, satisfied with the embers, he resettled himself in the fortified position and watched placidly as a car approached and stopped. A young woman got out, walked to the rear and opened the door of the horse trailer she had been towing.

"Well, well. Look-a-here." Doctor Doyle breathed, seeing the contrary black stallion emerge.

"Did you doubt me, my friend?" Replied a voice from inside the barn.

"I never doubt you."

"Then, I assume Mrs. Coleman is here with her new horse. The one with hind-quarters like a piston." He mocked in a caustic tone.

The ever-present German Shepherd bared his teeth in a menacing snarl as he ran to stand ground next to Doctor Doyle.

"Quiet, Dusty." A command resounded from the barn. "Bensen, help Mrs. Coleman with her horse."

There was a rustle from the loft, a few raining blades of hay and the stocky dwarf appeared outside.

John Hamil, too, came out of the barn while Bensen led As-Fault up the ramp. He rubbed the horse's muzzle and smiled for the first time in months.

As-Fault tossed his heavy mane and whinnied loudly, sending Dusty in retreat behind the heels of his master.

"Put him in a stall, Bensen, and tell Mrs. Coleman I'll begin his training in the morning. She is not to come by for two days, then I'll be ready to work with her." Abruptly he turned into the darkness of the barn.

Bensen did as he was bid, leaving Ellen alone with the veterinarian, who was still mutely planted in the entranceway. For a few moments she shuffled her feet awkwardly in the sandy ground, then, realizing that she had been dismissed, drove off.

Doctor Doyle drew deeply on his briar and exhaled two circlets of smoke, one through the other.

***

It was almost one o'clock on Thursday. Marisa had been sitting on the white fence that surrounded Ellen's corral since ten-thirty. There was no nail polish left of her new manicure; she'd chewed it all off. It had been an endless week with As-Fault at Hamil Farm. At last, Ellen's car and trailer rounded the bend and turned into her driveway. Marisa tried to appear calm. How could she be calm, knowing where she had sent As-Fault? To that demon Hamil, who would pole him as she had seen him do to Cinnamon and bruise his ribs as Scorpio's had been in a lesson to jump higher, even higher.

She pictured Scorpio's wounded belly and the dried blood matting his coat. Nevertheless, that punishment is what she counted on, for what she had laid the groundwork. According to Bobby Oakes – a seasoned trainer, *'a horse has a better memory than an elephant'*. She counted on his word. She was sorry As-Fault was made to suffer, but he wasn't alone. He would get retribution. So would Scorpio, and Rose-Marie. There were countless names on the list of Hamil's victims, hers included. Marisa believed As-Fault, like herself, had a deep rooted hatred. The seeds were planted; by August they will have grown to maturity.

Ellen stopped the car, but didn't open the door

Marisa arranged her face into a pleasant expression. "Good morning. I've been waiting for over an hour."

Still Ellen didn't open the door.

"Hey. Come on. I'm anxious to see an exhibition from you two."

Ellen stepped out lead-footed.

"You look tired, El'. I bet you two had a workout. I'll unload him. Go in and try my coffee. I made a fresh pot for you while I was waiting.

"Marisa…"

"Yes?" A bright smile.

"Marisa, As-Fault, he…we did the course perfectly. All the obstacles were set to specifications for any advanced course in a horse show. Hamil wants us to sign up for Working Hunter. The class is open to both professional and amateur entrants. He says As-Fault can jump anything now. He wants me to come every week, sometimes twice, until August. What do you think, Marisa? What class should we enter?"

"I don't know, Ellen. Mr. Hamil knows better than I do. I think you should go along with him. I told you, you wouldn't be disappointed with As-Fault."

Ellen walked to the rear of the trailer and opened the door slowly.

Marisa led As-Fault down the ramp. "Ellen, what happened?" She asked, seeing the wounds on her horse's inner flank. "It's just like, just like Scorpio. Don't you remember, Ellen? You do remember?" Her eyes darkened as she watched Ellen's reaction.

Ellen pulled her saddle from the trunk of the car and replied evasively. "We did really well, Marisa. He didn't touch a fence. He didn't fault once."

"I'm sure he didn't." She gave As-Fault his lump of sugar and examined the wound. "Looks like someone has already treated this. I guess you didn't question Hamil?"

"No. I didn't. As-Fault is fine, you can see for yourself. Excuse me. I have to call Larry at the office. I'll be right out. Do you want anything?" She called over her shoulder before going inside.

"No. I'll be in after I turn him out." Marisa rubbed As-Fault's nose and felt his warm breath. The muscles on his back were trembling in rippling spasms. She hadn't seen him nervous like that since the first day at the swim farm. He tossed his head and nuzzled her like a child looking for a way to express his joy at being home. Marisa checked and cleaned each hoof with the pick she had in her pocket. Satisfied that there was no tenderness or symptom of cracking, she opened the gate and As-Fault capered into the paddock. Marisa stood by the fence watching him. After a few moments she turned her back. As-Fault stopped running mid-stride. She gave him a piece of sugar. As-Fault cantered around the corral. Marisa turned away. Again, As-Fault stopped; he stood perfectly still. She suppressed a smile and continued into the kitchen.

Ellen had been watching by the sink. "Why does he stop so abruptly when you turn away?"

"Does he?"

"Yes. I saw from the window. He stops when you turn your back."

Marisa sat at the table. "He might have thought I was leaving." She pushed aside a large ashtray spilling over the stale butts of Larry's cigarettes. "Can't you get your husband to cut down a little?" She said to change the subject.

Ellen countered defensively. "Don't you get tired of wearing black and carrying that creepy walking stick? You don't use it."

The water was running in the sink. Marisa made no rejoinder.

Before going home, she brought As-Fault into the barn. He stood watching as she mucked out his stall and piled it high with straw and bedding so that it was dry and sweet smelling and easy on his feet.

***

On the first of each month, the secretary of the
Rotary Club posted the roster of scheduled activities
for the following month; and so, July first saw Ellen
Coleman eagerly seeking the official date set for her
breakfast affair. She was anxious to give the
information to the printer, to have the formal
invitations addressed and mailed promptly. Ellen
hoped it would be in the beginning of the month so
she would be free to use the remaining days to
sharpen her performance on As-Fault for the show
at Hamil Farm, the twenty-first of August. She was
totally unprepared for the two events falling on the
same date but there it was, clearly printed: HONOR
BREAKFAST, AUGUST 21, CHAIRMAN: MRS.
LARRY COLEMAN. She ran into the office.

"Can't we change the date?" She pleaded
with the secretary.

"I'm sorry, Ellen. I know I told you it
would be in the beginning of the month but a large
number of our members will be away at a National
Convention in Chicago. There are no other
openings on the calendar; see for yourself." She
pushed the page of squared off days scrawled with
red ink under her nose. "I hope you aren't
inconvenienced, but it's the only date I can give
you." The telephone on her desk rang and she
turned her attention away from Ellen.

Ellen left the office. What could she do? There was no way she could relinquish her position as chairman. Larry was being honored and she had to be there. She would have to forget about the horse show. 'Forget about it?' She had worked hard. She would lose face with Hamil. If she won a blue ribbon on As-Fault with everyone knowing Hamil had trained the horse and rider, she would certainly gain his recognition. There wouldn't be another opportunity to ride a horse like As-Fault in a points show. If she and As-Fault did as well in the show as in lessons they couldn't be beaten. She simply had to ride in that show at Hamil Farm on August twenty-first, the last week-end of the month, the last show before Hunt Season opened. She also had to make her husband proud of her as a hostess. She must find a way to do both. Marisa would help her. For some reason, this show meant as much to Marisa as it did to her.

Marisa and As-Fault were playing in the corral when Ellen arrived home. She stood by the car to watch. What a splendid horse he was: sleek and steel muscled under Marisa's constant care. It seemed they were playing 'Indian Chief.'. All kids played that game at one time or another; she smiled at the remembrance. One person is Chief, and the others do what the Chief does. The object is for a newcomer to figure out who is the leader. Marisa shook her head; As-Fault shook his head. Marisa kicked the ground with her foot; As-Fault pawed the dirt with his front hoof. She skipped and he pranced. Marisa was the Indian Chief. She turned her back and As-Fault stopped; he stood still. Marisa laughed, patted her playmate and gave him a lump of sugar. Ellen found it amazing, As-Fault didn't have to be worked hard to prevent him from becoming restless and having temperamental outbursts; all he required was Marisa's attention.

"Morning." Ellen called cheerlessly.

"Hi, El'. Today's the first. Did you get your date confirmed for the breakfast?"

"August twenty-first."

"Don't be funny. When is it?"

"August twenty-first and that's no joke."

The dull expression on Ellen's face told Marisa that surely she was not kidding. "Couldn't you get the date changed? There's plenty of time."

"I tried. The calendar is full." Her breaking point was near to the surface.

"What time does the breakfast start?"

Ellen answered glumly. "Ten o'clock."

"And what time is it over?"

"Oh, by the time they finish eating and giving out the awards, plus the speeches, I imagine they'll be through at one o'clock. I have to be there to see Larry receive the award and make his acceptance speech.

"Yes. You must be there." Marisa pushed her hair from her eyes. "I'll think of something." She said to fortify Ellen as they sat on the gate watching As-Fault nibble the buds on the blossoming Honeysuckle bush that spilled over the fence.

218

And think she did - all the way home in the car, through the night with Warren's back against hers. Her eyes were open watching the shifting designs on the ceiling cast by the lace window curtains. By the first prying rays of morning the plot was forming, by the time she reached Ellen's house it was resolved.

Ellen was exercising As-Fault. When she saw Marisa, she finished the figure-eight and trotted over to the fence.

Marisa was talking before Ellen could dismount. "If you program the award ceremony at the halfway point of the meal - an intermezzo before cake and coffee, - you will have heard Larry speak and everyone else by twelve o'clock. At that time the guests will be on dessert, milling around congratulating each-other and it wouldn't be impolite if you left. No one will notice. Larry can come to Hamil Farm later; he'll be able to watch you ride. He won't miss anything and you will have plenty of time to dress and be down on the field. What do you think?"

Ellen brightened. "You're right. I am the chairman. I could arrange it that way. There is nothing inappropriate. But how could I get As-Fault ready?" She removed his saddle and he cantered off to suck his fill of fresh water from the trough at the far end of the corral.

"That's easy. Bring As-Fault to Hamil Farm on Friday for your regular lesson. Leave him there overnight. You might even leave your riding clothes in your locker. Hamil shouldn't mind; he has plenty of vacant stalls." She surmised this, knowing

Hamil had been blackballed from the Hunt. Plus, the many awakened by *Leslie Allen's* articles had moved their horses elsewhere.

Ellen sighed, not thinking to question Marisa. How she knew the conditions of Hamil's barn was of no interest to her. She listened, hearing only that it was possible for her to be in that horse show.

Marisa went on. "You'll explain the situation to Hamil and ask him to please have As-Fault saddled and readied early that morning. Give him your credentials and ask him to register you and As-Fault in the Working Hunter Class, that you'll be there in time to ride. I'm sure he's done it for others, that way you'll be signed in well before the lists for registration close. Tell him that your friend will telephone you and tell you when to come. But don't let him know or even think that I'll be there. Don't mention my name But he won't ask." She said emphatically. "The Working Hunter Class starts after Junior Equitation on the flat. I'll call you when they start. You know the kids are slow and then the jump course has to be set up.   So, as I said, you have lots of time to change into riding clothes and bring As-Fault onto the field. Just inform the secretary at The Club that you're expecting an important message and where to find you. But I'll call you on the Cell phone first. You might have to turn off the ringer, can't chance letting a phone call interrupt a speech."

"I think it will work." Said Ellen, greatly relieved. She knew Marisa would find a solution. "The beginners on the flat show first. There's no jumping. Then there are at least two categories over fences before the Hunter Classes. That gives me, plenty of time. I think it will work. It will work." She sighed again.

"Yes, but don't come before you hear from me. There are always delays. You should enjoy the beautiful affair you arranged." Marisa put her arm on her friend's shoulder.

"Do you think As-Fault would play Indian Chief with me?"

"Why don't you try?"

Ellen thought a moment and then tossed her head so her hair whipped into her face. She turned to see if As-Fault would swing his long mane, but he bent the magnificent bow of his neck down to savor the young clover. "I guess not. You're the only Chief. Oh, Marisa, I forgot to tell you. Someone left a parcel here for you. It was by the front door when I went out this morning. It has no stamp and no return address, just your name, so it didn't come in the mail. I'll get it for you."

After leaving Ellen's house, Marisa pulled the car to the curb and took the small package out of her handbag. With trembling fingers and with characteristic curiosity, she unwrapped the layer of brown paper, and then the floral tissue, remembering Mac's story of the decapitated rat that had come to his office. But this box was long and narrow with the seductive promise of jewelry; there was nothing sinister about it. When she removed the paper, she saw a gray velvet jewelry box. Inside was a simple gold necklace – a twenty-four carat gold chain of flat woven links that would rest just below the cleft at her throat. It was an elegant piece that once clasped could remain there, lovely but not ostentatious. Beneath the necklace was a folded piece of paper. She opened it and read:

Dearest Marisa,

I want to fasten this on you myself, so you will know you carry my love always. Just let me meet you; wear this for me. That is all I ask, my love. I won't let it be over for us, Marisa. I won't!
Brad

He would not let her go. He might be watching her now. She looked in the mirror, locked the doors, put the box in her bag and sped home to Warren. Oh, thank God she had told him. He'd know what to do.

CHAPTER 14

John Hamil climbed the stairs to his bedroom. The
banister was in need of varnish where the raw wood
was exposed from wear. He was weary.
Margaret's deterioration and endless sniveling, plus
his own declining self-esteem plagued him.
Mundane nonsense: the irritating problems of men,
women and children, hounded him daily. Gossip
travels faster than the plague and Hamil Farm was
faring poorly under the affliction. The house was
unusually quiet for a Sunday morning. He recalled
he hadn't seen Margaret when he went out to the
barn but it had been later than usual. There wasn't
much work these days. All the Hunt members had
moved their horses to other stables since he *retired*
as Master. He referred to his dismissal from the
Hunt as *retirement,* refusing to admit to himself the
true reason. Those mewing cowards, they followed
him when there were brilliant crumbs of his fame to
peck on. Now they made excuses for their own
clumsiness and blamed him. '*Fools.*' Was it his
fault that they took a jump too wide and fell or
whatever else happened to the incompetent
wretches? 'People take up riding as a pass-time

without thinking of it as an Art that requires vigorous practice and discipline to perfect. I give them the opportunity to acquire that unison of movement. If it's not in the heart even their money can't buy it. *Fools*.'

He opened the door to the bedroom and caught a glimpse of himself in the pier mirror. 'A foul image for one deserving stars.' He swore. A thought passed his mind. He tried to repress it; nevertheless, it remained and continued to prick him. 'Damn Rose-Marie. If she had been paying attention, she would have been prepared for Cinnamon's sudden movement and controlled her horse as I taught her. She was supposed to win the Equestrian title for me. Then, how the name Hamil would be revered. Rose-Marie is dead but that doesn't pardon her error. Margaret? She's probably out hanging the wash. Better that I don't see her, her with eyes always persecuting me.' He muttered, dropping his thick gloves beside his muddy boots and going into the bathroom.

Tepid water drizzled out of the shower spigot with barely enough power to rinse off the suds that slid over his buttocks and down his legs. 'Didn't I tell Margaret to fix this,' he thought irritably, while scrubbing his body with a long handled brush until the skin was red and scratched from the stiff bristles. He examined his hands and lathered up his special cosmetic brush to buff his cuticles. His virgin fingers were tender and sensitive even to the softest nylon fibers designed for a woman's complexion. At last he was satisfied that all traces of a man who sweated and worked with his hands were divested of him. He had lived in this country long enough to learn that there is an unspoken class system determined by money or at least the appearance of having money that gains status. What you do and how well you do it were secondary to that elite social group that would accept you as a peer. It was the same in his country. In Belgium, he thought that he was accepted by the elite, was one of them. But for the disgrace of his rejection from the Olympic Team, he would have proved it. After that he severed his allegiance with the land, and burying all his yesterdays, left quickly, cynically taking a Flanders woman to wife - a woman who would give him his due respect and see to his needs, a woman whose ample hips held the promise of sons.

He knew little of America, only that it was a large free country on the map separated from Belgium by more than an ocean. America was young in comparison to Europe in the masterful training of horses; in America he would make a place for himself. Now, after years of being a property owner and a star among men, he was assured of his good standing - until *Leslie Allen*.

He was hungry. It annoyed him that there were no cooking smells coming from the kitchen. Something was amiss. It was too quiet, and 'where was Margaret?' She hadn't been in the bed when he came upstairs late in the night and he didn't see her this morning when he got up. She had taken to sleeping in Rose-Marie's room, which didn't bother him except when he expected her services as he did last night. But she should have made the bed for him and picked up his soiled clothes from the floor. 'Damn her,' he expected breakfast. Nude, he walked across the bedroom and opened his closet door. He stood straight: feet together, arms at his sides. After a moment he took a stride forward, removed the scarlet Hunt coat from the hanger and laid it on the bed. Then he began to dress himself: left leg into his briefs, then the right; he put his stockings and breeches on in the same manner, the white shirt – left arm, then the right. Extending his arms, he listened to the swishing sound his fine hands made as they moved along the silk lining of the Hunt coat and felt vitality spread to his extremities. The tall black boots added to his feeling of power. He set the silk hat on his head. The transformation complete, he faced the mirror. The image pleased him; his face contorted to barbaric austerity.

There was a knock at the door. He froze. 'Yes, the knock once again.' No one had ever dared to disobey his instructions and intrude on his sanctuary.

Once more, the knock.

"John, I must speak to you. Now, please." It was Margaret's voice from behind the locked door.

Shocked at her audacity, his anger curdled to fury. He opened the door and stared at a woman he barely recognized. She wore the fashionable tweed skirt and jacket of the Hunt Club women, the ones he'd looked at, never venturing to touch. Shining blond hair fell just short of her shoulders and curled softly to frame her face. It was a delicate face, not associated in his mind with the weary countenance of his wife. Margaret? She was the drab scuttling presence that cleaned, polished, set things in order – two scrawny dung colored braids atop her head, the bib of an apron pinned to a faded housedress. Margaret? This lady had a blush to her cheeks and rouged lips. Unconsciously, he removed his hat. They stood in the doorway glaring at one another in wonder – as strangers. Margaret never knew what her husband did behind the closed door. And he? He had never looked at Margaret, the woman – his wife. She was deceiving him, as had her hips. If he had had sons... Fury distorted his face. He raised his hand to slap her.

She didn't flinch. "I'm not alone, John, you can't hurt me."

He heard a creak on the staircase, eyed her suspiciously and stepped backward into the room, his grandeur fallen way to foolishness. It was her manner, the poise in one ordinarily so docile, that disarmed him. The rage mounted; he tried to close the door.

"Leave the door open." She instructed. Then verbalizing the significance of his costume added: "Didn't the Hunt begin early this morning as usual?" It was a sarcastic dig to ridicule him.

He looked at her hatefully. She knew he hadn't joined The Chase since October.

Adrenaline pumped through her body, making her effective for the first time since her marriage. Years of fear and resentment that went so deep as not to be identified erupted. Her eyes narrowed. "I'm divorcing you, John."

He stood still, said nothing. In confused desperation he looked in the mirror for reassurance.

"These are my terms: Hamil Farm is mine – the house and the land." She saw his eyelids quiver, his brows come together as he glared at her. "The horses are yours. I want no alimony. You can have the horse show here in August as scheduled. You can continue with your lessons here until then, that's the end of the show season. Then, I don't want to see you or your man, Bensen, again. And John, …you will be out of *my* house by dinnertime tonight."

Her last words stopped him. Silence, except for her heart that she could hear booming in her chest.

He leapt at her with a yowl of attack that did not sound human, that ended in an insane wail as the hand that would pummel her was caught in mid-air.

"John, this is Donald Posey. We will be married as soon as the divorce comes through."

The barrel-chested man now had hold of both Hamil's hands and pushed him to the bed; his knees gave way and he sank down heavily.

Margaret was speaking Flemish. "The deed to the Farm is in my name. I don't think you will cause me any trouble, because if you do you'll go to jail; I'll inform the authorities how you swindled the insurance company to get the money you needed to kill my daughter." She was sobbing uncontrollably, hysterical now, clutching at her own hands until she could no longer hold herself. "MURDERER, MURDERER MURDER. YOU KILLED HER.

YOU KILLED ROSE-MARIE." She sprung at him, clawing at his face, as he sat helplessly restrained on the bed.

Posey pulled her away, while still gripping Hamil with one hand. He hadn't understood a word of the foreign conversation, but saw the need to act. "Stop now, Honey. It's okay."

Blood streamed from four long gashes on John Hamil's cheek. One of her fingernails had caught and ripped the bottom lid of his right eye; it appeared that the spinning eyeball would funnel out of the red socket, He didn't see Donald Posey and Margaret leave the room, but sat on the bed staring at the open door.

"Be out by eight o'clock tonight." He heard Margaret say firmly, then the tap of her high heels going down the stairs.

***

It was evening when Marisa was driving over the bridge toward Charleston, toward home where she hoped Warren would be waiting for her. She wanted to show him the necklace Brad had left for her and the note. She hoped he would find a way for them to be free of him. She always considered herself an intelligent woman who had control of her life, not a fool to find herself in the midst of the age-old cliché of a lover's triangle that always leads to desperation - the stuff of movies and novels. She could have turned away from Brad as well as she could have said 'no' to her ego and turned away from Hamil; the choices were hers and now she was trapped and saw no way out. She wished she were able to focus on the magnificence of the sunset: vibrant colors streaking across the sky spilling over the harbor, sparkles of light. 'Certainly more awesome than John Hamil riding a horse through the woods'. She remembered how hypnotized she was that morning watching from the hilltop. Funny, she thought, how she could pinpoint the day – the minute that altered the course of her life. Oh, there were warning signals, many, but she didn't heed them; they would only get in her way. So, she covered them with her *comfort blanket* – denial. 'Bad things happen to other people, not to me.'

Warren was on the balcony with a bunch of roses in his hand when Marisa pulled the Corvette into the garage. She leaned on her cane as she climbed the stairs to greet him. Her spirits were down in contrast to his, which soared. His eyes were lit from a happiness that she knew only success could ignite. She smiled when he put the roses in her arms. He was so pleased and anxious to tell her the news of his signing the long awaited contract. There had been far too many pit falls, what with Raittown's bankruptcy, her accident and the disappointment of As-Fault's promising racing career. Now, Warren proclaimed, it was time for them to celebrate the good times.

It would be a party, he told her. Chez and Anna were coming for dinner. Anna insisted on bringing her specialty –eggplant lasagna. Chez would bring his hearty appetite. It would be like old times, only better because Chez was settled; he and Anna had set their wedding date in September. The future was mapped out at a pace that would balance the cash flow. The construction jobs would be creative and lucrative. Instead of *Raittown*, the housing developments were called *Plantation Villas, Inc.* Warren had become a conservative; being pompous only caused financial demise and almost cost him his wife.

Warren spun Marisa around in his arms and kissed her, then put the signed contract down on the table and slapped his hand on the open pages. "We did it. The bank finally gave us financing for two projects north of Camden. Twenty houses each, small, but it's a start."

He danced with her in his arms, spinning and laughing and for the moment she was caught up in his joy. Round and round, her head was spinning, she grasped his neck and begged him to stop. The floor came up to join the ceiling - vertigo like after the accident, like before she fell into the pool at the swim farm. Her slack body was heavy in his arms and he set her down on the chair. Marisa wiped the beads of perspiration from her forehead.

"I haven't felt this way in months."

"It's my fault. Lie down for a while. I'll set the table. Tonight will be a celebration!"

Lying in the tub with the door open, she listened to Warren moving about downstairs. She had to do something about the necklace in the box. Brad would not let up. He was still a threat to her marriage, to Warren and perhaps even to himself. Never before was she unable to unscramble life's puzzles. Never before had she been one to rely on another to make her decisions. She was so sure of herself, so cocky in her independence and now she felt as if her feet were not on solid ground. Warren was being all she ever wanted him to be, all he promised that evening at dinner in the bistro. She loved him so, more now than ever since they recommitted to each other. She could not doubt his sincerity.

Soon the vertigo passed, she relaxed and was looking forward to the evening. She dried herself and put on the red caftan he admired, pinned up her hair the way he liked it and went downstairs, leaving the box on the bedside table. Warren would know what to do about it, she'd ask him after dinner. She wouldn't sabotage Warren's happiness tonight.

Later, she read the contracts and tried to make her enthusiasm sound sincere. In truth it was; she was proud of her husband and relieved that he no longer looked at himself as a failure. She shared his joy but all the while her mind was tormented by the thought of the gray velvet box, the necklace, and the threat it implied.

Marisa was clearing the dinner table. Anna stood to help her. Chez handed up a stack of plates. "Did you know Hamil Farm is up for sale? His wife put it on the market this morning." He said.

Marisa drew a breath of surprise. "How do you know?"

Warren refilled his wine glass. "Marisa, property is our business."

"He'll never allow it. At Hamil Farm he's a legend."

"Well, I tried calling him at home. No one answered. Then I remembered that his Cell number was in our phonebook. He answered. When I asked for information he began ranting and blubbering that it's not true, Hamil Farm was not for sale. He wouldn't make an appointment for me to see the grounds; actually he ordered me to stay away. He sounded desperate."

She went into the kitchen calling over her shoulder, "He'll never sell. Don't waste your time."

"He has no choice. It seems Hamil Farm doesn't belong to him. It belongs to his wife. Anyway, it won't happen before his show there, and, the ground is too hilly for housing. With that steep incline and low lying field, there would always be plumbing problems."

After Chez and Anna went home Warren helped Marisa clean up the kitchen. When they went upstairs he looked at her quizzically having been aware of her forced smile all evening.

Without a word she handed him the box.

Warren opened it, read the note then folded it and replaced it inside. His face was expressionless, only his jaw tightened. He put the box in his pocket. "I'll handle this."

"But what should I do?"

He was standing next to the bed, she, on the other side, not knowing how she could lie beside him with this snowball grinding down upon them.

"He's relentless, Warren. He's following me always; I'm sure of it. My God, if he tells Hamil about the notes in the car. That man's a lunatic; he…"

"I said, I'll take care of it."

"But how?"

"We won't speak of it again." His voice was authoritative. "I won't let either of them spoil another moment for us. I can't even bring myself to say their names. I know how hard you've worked with Ellen to get As-Fault ready for that horse show. Of course you'll go to watch. After that, not a word. Agreed?"

Marisa nodded but she was uneasy when she went to bed. Warren held her in his arms; she felt his body warm and close and soon fell asleep.

Warren slept soundly; there was even a hint of a smile on his lips.

***

Much of the success of the record companies can be attributed to the talents of poor southern blacks. They were paid a pittance, perhaps a used pink Cadillac, for their music that made the record companies billions. Brad may speak combatively to the powerful bosses at meetings but as an *indie,* an independent promoter not affiliated with a production company, he never damaged his cultivated relationships with artists and disc jockeys. He established faith with each individual personally, for without the deejay there is no ear for the music. And the record companies knew that without the indies there were no deals and no money. It went up and down the ladder from there to the head of Sonic Records, whose agent for the *Galaxy* album was Brad Novick.

Since his affair with Marisa, his attitude had changed. He had bad-mouthed, in fiery language, to Irv Herman for not airing one of the songs in the *Galaxy* album because, as the deejay said, the words were racist and inciting.

"Choose another cut in the album." Herman urged. "I'm responsible for the records I play. If you don't like it other indies will buy the air space." *'To hell with Brad Novick.'*

Common sense told Brad that if he were to go on as a functioning individual he must erase Marisa from his mind. This obsession was jeopardizing his reputation in business and making him a nasty person inwardly. He had broken up with many women who loved him. Some held on in hope of reconciliation but he avoided them; after a while they gave up. If not, he found cruel pleasure at seeing how much rejection and humility they would endure; almost as a cat toys with a mouse. He knew he must forget Marisa. But he couldn't. Just seeing her kept her in his life. He looked for her car in the parking lot of the Inn each time he returned. Tonight, for an elated moment, he thought he saw her Corvette but it was Ol'Mo's pickup truck; he often stayed for supper after his work on the grounds.

Lonely and tired, he went up to his room, dropped his pile of mail on the bureau and went into the bathroom to wash his face, then taking a beer from the mini-fridge, sat down in the one easy-chair. After a long swig he began to go through the letters and magazines. There was always a lot of junk mail. Carelessly, he ripped open the envelopes: bills, announcements and invitations. One looked like a greeting card. As he opened it something dropped onto his lap. It was the necklace he had sent to Marisa. Holding the gold chain in his hand, he opened the sweet smelling Hallmark Card. On the cover was a nostalgic watercolor picture. It might have been the pond outside his window. In the picture were two lovers, their arms around each other, beneath a Willow Tree. Inside was a note written with Marisa's familiar flourish - slanted as were the notes he had seen in her journal - rushed off in the hand of a reporter, but he read without any trouble.

Dear Brad,

Yes, I think of you always. Perhaps I'm looking for an excuse to see you. Understand my fears but I want so much to wear the beautiful necklace to feel you warm next to me. I can't refuse myself that. My heart is beating rapidly now just thinking of the beauty of our coming together. Meet me at Hamil's barn at six o'clock, Saturday morning on August 21st. I'll be there to prepare As-Fault for the show. I know it's early but we can be alone. Please, don't try to see me until then, My Love, it could spoil everything; I will be there. Wear my necklace close to your body for me. Two months, Darling, it will all be sorted out in two months.

    M.

He went to the mirror, fastened the necklace around his neck and smoothed the links against his skin. Anxiously, he reread the message remembering how difficult it was to decipher Marisa's journal because she didn't dot her 'I's. Having memorized the words, he folded the note and put it in his wallet. Had he looked carefully, he would have seen that here the letter 'T' was carefully crossed and didn't run across the word.as in the journal. The "I" too was easily distinguished. But he was heedless of the writing; the meaning he secured in his heart. He would try not to see her, telling himself that the next time he looked upon her face she would be wearing the necklace, and would be his.

CHAPTER 15

Two months. Never in his life had Brad used time so frugally; it was the first time he was working to create a life for someone else. He was focused on a life with Marisa. He chose to be left alone. It was a right he protected and allowed the same respect to others as well, but Marisa had told him not to see her until August twenty-first., two months - an eternity.

He tried. He sat alone in restaurants and watched couples laughing and touching, absorbed in each other, unmindful of the rest of the world. He went to movies and ate popcorn alone. He arranged his visits to radio stations and auditions so he was close to the Inn and able to sleep the night in the bed he had lain with Marisa.

His love took on the quality of worship. He was devout to one purpose - to create a life with Marisa. He tried to stay away as she had bid. He tried, but it was impossible, only now he was more discreet. He watched from afar and wore a baseball cap and baggy clothing. On occasion, he rented a car, and sat invisible, all the while fingering the gold chain around his neck. The necklace was a link between them. In the past, whenever he visited a museum, he would wait until the guard turned his back then touch his favorite sculpture or artifact experiencing the same sensation the artist had during its creation. So it was with the necklace. It put time in another perspective and gave him the patience he needed to get by. Each day was a day closer to Marisa. She had called him '*My love*', it filled his spirit. Nothing would stop him from making their union a commitment forever.

***

AUGUST 21,

Brad figured he would wake up at four o'clock in the morning and be at Hamil Farm before dawn, before the final preparations for the horse show got underway. He was convinced that Marisa was in danger. This he held as fact - a clash between Hamil and Marisa meant imminent harm to her. He hadn't told anyone about her being *Leslie Allen* as he had threatened. Perhaps by now Hamil, himself, figured out her secret identity. Yet there was another reason for this ominous premonition. It gnawed at him and gave him no rest. *'Hamil was bent on Marisa's destruction and only he could prevent it'.*

It was well after midnight when Brad finished dining with friends but he wasn't tired; in his business he kept *'Vampire Hours'*. Nevertheless, he had been careful not to have more than one glass of wine during the evening and was afraid that if he rested for even a little while, he might not wake in time. Instead of sleep, he took a shower and put on the freshly pressed Levi's that Mrs. Sanderson had left in the closet for him. Thank Goodness for that blessed lady; she was the only one who bothered about him. Even when she baked cookies in the kitchen with her grandchildren, she always remembered him. He'd come back to the Inn to find a plate of Toll House cookies and a glass of milk on the bureau. Tonight that kindness didn't satisfy the emptiness in his chest.

Despite the hour, Brad decided to drive over to Hamil Farm and wait in his car until daybreak. At such an early hour he knew no one would be there; it was the best opportunity for a confrontation with Hamil.

The streets were empty when he started out. Low lying clouds hid the moon. '*So dark. Was this venture madness?*' Either his efforts would be heroic or he would make a clown of himself; he had to do something. Marisa was so excited when she spoke about Hamil Farm, all in superlatives. He warned her that she had become an adrenaline junkie, getting high on the thrill of jumping horses and challenging her fears. It was drama out of proportion. He'd seen the man. John Hamil didn't appear frightening. He looked like any other man who worked from dawn to dusk on the land and with animals, and not a particularly strong man at that with the limp and all.

Country lanes appear different at night. He drove slowly, though he had been there many times and knew his way. The car's headlights didn't penetrate the opaque mist hovering over the road. He leaned forward, peering through the windshield. He'd been driving for an hour. Assuming he must have passed the farm, he turned the car around and backtracked. He was tired. All week he lay in bed at night watching the ceiling, creating scenarios that would transpire with Marisa beside him. '*My Love*' - she had written those words. She called him, '*My*

241

Love.' More than anything, he yearned for the fulfillment of the words and the sentiment of that note to become his life. '*My Love.*' Brad was impatient. He rubbed his eyes. It wasn't a good idea, after all, he realized, not to sleep.

The road turned. He looked for a familiar landmark – a stone wall, a gate. The trees had been without foliage in January, the last time he was there. Now, during the summer, everything was overgrown. There was the constant mist and stench of a decaying bog. He drove on cautiously. A gust of wind, the fog swelled, rolled and parted. '*Ah there's, the barn.*' It was easier to see coming from the opposite direction. '*Yes, that's the weathervane on the cupola. It would glitter in the sunlight during the day but tonight was so very dark.*'

He decided to park by the roadside until morning; he'd sleep for a while and feel better. He turned off the headlights, checked the door locks, and though the night was hot and uncomfortably humid, put up the windows. He didn't like the sound of the dog barking in the distance. '*So tired.*' He lay his head back; the dog stopped barking, now was only the silent screech of fear. Seeking comfort in the warmth of the necklace at his throat, he closed his eyes. Sleep soon shut out the noise.

Perhaps the sudden stillness woke him. Even before he opened his eyes to the burst of light he knew it wasn't the sun…he wasn't alone. A face was staring through the window, a face hideous

242

above the flashlight shining on heavy features and soot-blackened eyes barred by tangles of black hair. Brad gasped. The man, at full height, just reached the top of the car, yet the breadth of his shoulders was as wide as the door. Beside him was a German Shepherd, his forefeet on the window, saliva dripping from exposed fangs. The man laid a large red gasoline can on the hood of the car.

"Get out." He grunted, and shone the beam on the can and the gas torch he had in his other hand.

'Did he mean to ignite the can and blow up the car if he didn't obey?' Brad tried to explain the reason he was parked. Then, believing this a robbery, took his wallet from his pocket and offered it to him, thinking smugly how clever he'd been to leave the wad of cash he always carried for business stuffed inside a shoe in the closet at the Inn. The man took the wallet and lit the torch to it. In an instant it was ashes and fluttered away.

'If this isn't robbery, what else does this miserable dwarf want?' His mind was searching for another reason. "I'm sorry, I was tired and fell asleep. I didn't know this was private property. I'll move on now." He reached and turned the car key. The engine didn't catch. Disbelieving, he tried again only to hear a tinny click, click of the ignition. He looked questioningly at the dreadful face.

"Get out." The man turned off the flashlight. A blue flame licked the gas can, blistering the paint.

Brad opened the door and got out. He towered above his captor. The dog growled and lunged at him. Brad raised his arm to protect

243

himself, but the canine teeth caught on his sleeve and cut into his skin. Blood seeped through the shirt, ran down his arm over his hand.

"You walk."

Brad was sharply prodded forward. The dog tagged behind like a domestic pet out for an airing.

"Where are you taking me?" Brad protested in fright. "I had no intention of trespassing." He turned to appease his tormentor. All meaning dissolved in the black craters beneath protuberant brows. Brad's scalp prickled. He wiped the sweat from his forehead with the sleeve of his shredded shirt, unknowingly smearing blood across his face. 'This must be Bensen.' He recalled Marisa's description of the farm-hand and realized that argument was futile - Bensen was simply a servant acting under orders. He was being taken to John Hamil.

They continued walking to the barn, black and enormous in the gloom. Tall walls frowned down on a number of smaller structures that Brad hadn't noticed before. Bensen proceeded up the ramp to the great wooden door studded with iron spikes. No light appeared through the chinks. With surprising ease, Bensen swung the door outward, metal grinding on metal, and shoved him inside; there was a rush of cool air. The door slammed behind him. He could hear Bensen slide the outside latch. The dog whined for a moment, scratched to get in, then threw his weight against the door and slumped down in resignation.

He was alone in the engulfing blackness and unearthly stillness. shivering in spasms of hot and cold, while his stomach turned sour. His body felt damp and clammy. He hugged himself tightly disregarding the blood that still dripped from his arm. Brad had a phobia of darkness but he wasn't squeamish at the sight of blood. He was a skilled huntsman. A memory flashed across his mind.

It was getting dark. He had been perched, cramped in his tree-stand since pre-dawn wearing camouflage and stinking of fox urine to disguise his human scent. A twig snapped, a rustle in the bush and there browsing beneath him was a Buck with a magnificent twelve-point rack.

Soundlessly, he knocked his arrow, brought the compound bow up, fixed the target in the cross hairs of his telescopic sight and let fly. The arrow arced high in the air and found its' mark deep in the animal's chest but did not bring him down. He took off in a whirlwind of dust. Brad tracked the bloody trail on tall blades of grass and spots where it had soaked into the dry earth; with so much blood, he must have punctured a lung. Shadows were getting long when he finally found the gasping Buck by a fallen tree. He unsheathed his knife from his belt and gave the deer the coup de grace. Expertly, he separated the meat from the entails, which he left for scavengers. He skinned and butchered the carcass on site. When he was done, he wiped his blade on a hank of grass, then wrapped each steak in a plastic Baggie to distribute to his clients. The glorious antlers and hide he kept for himself. But Brad knew he was no match for the Buck; they hadn't gone cunning to cunning. He had merely ambushed a noble animal.

"I am John Hamil. I presume you want to see me." A hollow voice in the void was very near.

Brad put out his hand and groped in front of him. Someone caught his wrist. A light turned on. The naked bulb dangling from the high rafter illuminated a man dressed in the formal foxhunting attire Brad had seen so often in sporting magazines and paintings of the English countryside. The bulb swayed back and forth casting long quivering shadows across the floor. The man, himself, appeared to be oscillating and largely distorted having the quality of a hallucination. Nothing was authentic; Brad became disoriented and nauseated.

"You shouldn't have come here uninvited at night." He released Brad's hand.

The man framed in the uncertain light was less than an arm's reach before him. From what Brad could distinguish, he was lean, of average height with red-rimmed eyes that gleamed from under the high hat. The skin was fascinating. It was thick and leathery with a yellowish pallor, as of one who had lived a lifetime outside and was suddenly confined indoors away from health giving sunshine. Except the hands…they were white with long delicate fingers that seemed to possess an entity of their own. Brad tried to keep his imagination at bay. *'Imagination packs more wallop than logic.'* Logic told him that it was the hour that created oddities, that this was the meeting he had anticipated. He looked around to establish his whereabouts and found he was in the center of a broad aisle; he took a deep breath and stiffened his knees. Seen from afar Hamil had appeared to be a harmless farmer, not this menacing character in front of him.

Hamil reached up, steadied the bulb and stood within a cone of light. He chuckled. "With that blood on your face you look like you've had the ritual of your first Hunt."

Brad touched his face, wiped his soiled fingers on his jeans.

Light brought reality and with it Brad's confidence. In the stall beside him was a large black horse shuffling uneasily, tossing his head up and down.

Brad cleared his throat. "That must be As-Fault." Even in this alien place As-Fault carried an unmatched grandeur.

"As-Fault belongs to Ellen Coleman, a student of mine. She is to show him in the morning.

"His eyes narrowed. "I know why you're here. I told you on the telephone that you will never get my property. I told you not to come. No one can take it from me."

"You're mistaken. I never called; it wasn't me." Brad began to gesticulate wildly, as if he could pull an explanation from the air. He had come to threaten Hamil and now he was on the defensive. His words faltered then gained strength. "My only concern is Marisa Rait. That horse is As-Fault. He belongs to Marisa. She will be here." While concealed in the rented car, Brad had watched Ellen ride the horse in the corral at her house. It was obvious she was working him for Marisa and would ride him in the show. He wondered why Ellen hadn't told Hamil that As-Fault belonged to Marisa.

Hamil chuckled, slapping his boot with the riding crop he held. "Ahh, Marisa Rait? How is she? The girl has not been here since her fall. Too bad, she was a promising rider, but conceit and ambition took away her judgement. It will be nice to see her again." The sang-froid intonation of his voice had a meaning other than the words spoken.

"Mr. Hamil, I don't know you. I don't want your property. Your business is horses. I know business - all the deceitful maneuvers." As-Fault, he concluded, was the crux of this matter. "Be advised if anything happens to Marisa I have enough evidence of fraud and endangerment to have you convicted. You'll be locked to a chain gang and made to dig ditches with your virgin hands. You hurt her once, I won't let you hurt her again."

Empowered by his words, he was fully recovered from his fright. It was obvious that John Hamil was an eccentric living here in the barn with the horses. In the next stall was a sleeping area fashioned out of bales of hay and covered with a plaid horse blanket; a heap of brown clothing and muddy boots were piled against the rough boards. On top of the heap, resting on a pillow was a blond haired doll. He didn't have time to wonder about that.

"I'll be leaving now. Kindly tell your man outside to repair my car. I mean you no harm. I'm not here to buy Hamil Farm or take anything from you, I only wish to protect Marisa Rait. You do understand me, don't you?"

"Your friend Marisa is of no importance to me. I told you when you called to stay away. You should have listened."

"I didn't call you."

"We've been working through the night in preparation for the horse show tomorrow and then Sunday morning is the last Hunt of the season. It will be a drag hunt across Hamil Farm, and because this is my property it is my job to lay the scent. We don't hunt foxes anymore." He idly flicked a piece of lint from his sleeve.

"I tell you, it wasn't me who called."

"Bensen is getting ready now to tow the meat along the course for the hounds to follow. I believe you'll have no more trouble with your car." He called to Bensen but his eyes remained on Brad's face. "Take care of our guest."

A grating sound. Bensen had pulled open the door; his bosky shape appeared grossly huge in the entrance."

"Good-night." Hamil's steely eyes forbade reproach. He reached up and switched off the current.

"Please, I don't want your property." Brad tripped stepping backward.

Bensen yanked him up and pushed him outside.

"You don't understand; I don't want your property." Pleading back into the darkness.

The dog stood expectantly; with tail wagging, he sniffed at Brad's crotch before trotting ahead in the pale circlet of light cast by Bensen's following flashlight.

Brad had never known the kind of terror that was closing in on him. He was unprepared for the severity of the physical symptoms of fear. His stomach convulsed into lurching upheavals that rose in his throat and dropped down to his bladder, he was afraid he would wet himself. He could smell his own fear. Animals, he knew, can smell a man's fear.

Stumbling, half running, the driveway seemed endless. It was impossible to differentiate the ringing in his ears from the chirping of the multitude of cicadas. He lost his footing and fell into a water filled pothole onto a rusting coil of barbed wire which ripped his trousers and cut his shins to bloody ribbons. '*So many obstacles,*' He kept his head down. When they came to the bend in the roadway he looked up. "My car is gone. Where is my car?"

The beam from the flashlight went out. In the blinding darkness Brad was overcome by the visage of inescapable doom – the counting down of one's final minutes.

The dog snarled, the hairs along his spine stiffened. He whipped around to face Brad with eyes red as burning coals, with barred teeth – polished prongs erect in gaping jaws. To fend off the coming attack Brad swung his arms around to grab Bensen and hoist him over his head. He forgot Bensen's lack of height and his arms flailed at air as the dog hurled himself onto his chest. Hot canine breath torched his cheek before the long teeth plunged into his neck. An icy pain paralyzed him; his eyes bulged. Choking and gasping, he was drowning in the blood that gurgled from his nose and mouth. The dog was tearing at his flesh. The light flashed on and for an instant, through a warm scarlet sea, Brad saw the lurid face of Bensen. He fell to the ground. His last sight was of the gold necklace; it had been ripped from his throat and lay beside him in the mud. Then, he died.

Bensen pulled the dog away. Dusty whimpered and tugged to free himself, his teeth still gnashing to devour his kill.

"Go." Bensen grunted.

The dog slinked off to the barn.

Bensen stripped the body and dropped Brad's clothing into the underground incinerator a few feet away where the debris of the land was kept burning during Spring clean-up. The car would be swallowed in the swamp.

Dawn was pecking at the horizon. Soft, rosy hues crept over the meadow from the East, and Bensen had not yet completed his night's work. He rolled the body in sand to stop the bleeding and raked a layer of gravel over the telltale signs on the driveway. He then took Brad by the hair, lashed a chain under his chin, and under his armpits. From the small barn, he brought one of the school horses and mounted it. He reached down for the chain and kicked the horse. Bensen dragged the scent for the Hunt eight miles, back and forth across Hamil Farm, over the burr carpeted woods down by the beach, through the stinking sluice of yellow water that flowed from the deep swamp, leaving the unrecognizable prize for the hounds in the thicket hemming the high North Field. What the canines didn't devour would be eaten away by ants.

Vans were already arriving in the paddock when Dusty returned to his master. John Hamil was cordially designating hitching areas to the contestants. Bensen was ordered to the back barn.

There was no trace of the night visitor to Hamil Farm.

CHAPTER 16

Truth, as Marisa knew it, was that John Hamil was Evil personified. Service to the truth was good in itself. Her plan left no chance of failure. Today, the day of its' realization, she was calm. Nothing would prevent her from being at Hamil Farm for the horse show.

Warren told Marisa that the architect had arranged this Saturday to survey the new sites up North. He knew it was the day of the Horse Show but would be unable to reschedule until next month. "I'm sorry, Darling, I'll leave home early and meet you there on the way back. There's a good chance I'll be there before As-Fault's class." With words so sweet, so coaxing, he invited her to come with him knowing full well that no amount of tempting promises would keep her from being there with As-Fault.

Saturday morning. Marisa pretended to be asleep when Warren got out of bed. She had been watching the clock before dawn, hoping he would soon leave. She didn't want any more discussion about The Horse Show. They had made peace. She didn't want to risk his warning her not to go without him.

He was a long time in the shower. He sensed her tension and eyes on him as he dressed and moved about the bedroom. Finally, attired in his business suit, he was 'prepared to meet with his architect.'

"Good luck with As-fault today. See you later." He said after a perfunctory kiss on her cheek.

Barely a moment passed when he returned for his briefcase that he "forgot." She was already out of bed and so startled to see him that she jumped. Warren smiled to himself – it was a wonderful dramatic touch. He swore he could hear her sigh of relief as he went down the steps to his car. She would be at the window watching him drive away. Marisa, with all her anxiety and speed, would be an hour behind him.

He was on the highway before the traffic buildup. The sky was gray but there were dashes of color in the distance. He pulled into a truck-stop where he grabbed The Charleston Post and brought a cup of coffee and a buttered roll out to enjoy his car. While glancing through the morning edition he noted that MacGrath, was still writing the column that had been *Leslie Allen*'s spot. Mac wrote with more punch of the facts than with the empathy included in Marisa's style. Surely, there must be others who marked the difference.

Hamil Farm was a hubbub of activity. Spectators were directed to park in the paddock by the street where the fence had been taken down. Already it was pretty full but Warren found a hidden space between two vans and squeezed in. Marisa was probably cursing him for stalling and costing her time, plus the traffic that would have slowed her down. It was a mean trick, but her surprise and happiness in seeing him would be worth the brief annoyance. He genuinely did want to share As-Fault's victory with her.

It was a perfect day for an outdoor pageant. Judging by last night's foul weather, he doubted that today would be so favorable. Summer heat had abated and the air was invigorating. Warren walked slowly up the road leading to the barn. The place gave him a sickening feeling of déjà vu; this was the place where Marisa fell. In his mind's eye he saw her still hands on the hospital bed, he remembered how he had caressed her bruised cheek. He stopped walking and closed his eyes, overtaken by the consuming pain of the possible loss of his wife. Alone with his memory, he surrendered to the destiny of which he was part, knowing fully that he had begun to re-claim the dignity that had been stripped of him. Some men can live outside of their self-image. Warren was not one of them. He opened his eyes and continued up the road to the barn.

In the paddock opposite the farmhouse a chestnut mare was grazing while her sturdy foal nursed at her teat. The morning haze that lingered in the treetops had all but evaporated into the cloudless sky. To the innocent eye, all was well at Hamil Farm. Birds sang in the trees, a hawk soared the thermal air high above the fields. Warren watched him sail languidly then swoop down, maybe for an unsuspecting mouse, He glanced at his watch, twelve-thirty, lunchtime for that Red-tailed raptor.

Rounding the curve, a shimmering light caught his attention. He thought it was the sun dancing on the pools of rainwater amid the gravel, or perhaps it was something submerged that gleamed so brightly. He bent over to investigate, put his hand into the puddle and took out a gold chain. Warren tossed it up in the air, caught it in his palm and dropped it in his pocket. The corner of his lip quivered ever so slightly. He heard a car coming up the driveway behind him. He turned; *'it couldn't be Marisa quite yet,'* He quickened his step.

Warren wasn't surprised when he entered the barn that most of the horses were down on the field. No one was in the barn, neither was Ellen in the tack room. Only As-Fault was there saddled and tacked up. *'Hamil must have gotten him ready.'* A bag of riding clothes was hanging on the hook where As-Fault's bridle was kept. It was just as Marisa had said, *"Ellen would be there after the Rotary breakfast. It would be a shame if she were detained and unable to ride in the show."* He took the gold chain from his pocket, methodically wiped and polished it on his sleeve until it shone, then scratched a few lines on a piece of paper and put them together inside the gray velvet box which he had in his pocket. He laid the box on top of Ellen's Hacking Jacket in the bag.

Warren left the barn and went toward the show area. He stopped on the hillside, which overlooked the field, and sat down on a patch of dry grass to wait for Marisa. They would watch Ellen win a blue ribbon on As-Fault and then they would be done with Hamil Farm.

It was nine-thirty when Marisa sped onto the Interstate. She knew the first event had started but there was time. She accepted the profane gestures and snarls of road rage without looking back as she darted through the weekend traffic. At last, she put the Corvette into a four- wheel drift off the exit and rounded the corner onto the country road toward Hamil Farm. As-Fault would not have to be ready for another hour. Everything was on schedule. Ellen was waiting for her call. Marisa pictured her friend trapped at the Rotary Club Breakfast, biting her already torn cuticles. Ellen was nervous. *'Ellen was always nervous.'*

The tires grated on the dirt road; a cloud of dust billowed behind her. She accelerated, the wheels spun, gripped and she regained speed, driving directly eastward into the blinding sun. She pulled down the visor, and adjusted her sunglasses; it was impossible to see through the barrage of light. She leaned back and straightened her arms against the steering wheel while continuing to press the gas pedal.

From behind moss laden branches, a flash of red, a gash of black. *'A mirage, please, a mirage'.*

It swept into her blurred vision and streaked closer with increasing speed. Marisa rubbed her eyes. John Hamil riding As-Fault at full gallop down the narrow road was on a true collision course toward the car. His red coat and white ascot bore down on her.

"No, not As-Fault." She cried and swerved the speeding car off the road barely avoiding a fatal impact with her horse. She stood on the brakes. The heavy car slowed for an instant before it struck the embankment skirting the road. Slowly, the car rolled over onto its left side. The door crumbled on the roadway and the car flipped again onto its roof. Pressed against the rear of the seat, she watched as if detached, fascinated by her face in the rear view mirror. There was a lovely little crack and every piece of glass in the car broke simultaneously into a colony of spider webs. The Corvette sailed across the road.

"I'm going to die." Marisa said to the stranger, who was herself, looking out from the broken mirror. She was not afraid. She watched impending death. It was laggard in coming. Funny, she'd thought such a violent death would be quicker. She waited. The car struck a boulder, turned over and ceased moving. She was quite comfortable there inside. All was quiet, peaceful; time topped.

Someone was banging on the door.

'Why would anyone disturb her?'

A man with a crowbar was trying to open the door.

She turned her head away from the disturbing sound. She was so comfortable. 'Why should she move?'

"She's alive." The man shouted over the whirring of the engine and spinning wheels. "Miss, turn off the engine." His voice was insistent.

Marisa looked about, bewildered.

"The engine. Turn off the engine!"

'Who was he speaking to?'

"Turn off the key before a fire starts."

She coughed. Smoke was filling the cockpit; her eyes were tearing. *The key?* *Everything was upside down.*

"Did they get the body out?" Another voice called.

It was a young boy's voice; hearing it she thought of how she enjoyed playing Ringolevio with the boys in the schoolyard; giggling, she would let them 'capture' her. *'Boys'.* That was when she first noticed their existence. *'When was that...sixth grade?'* Her mind was wandering. She tried to get control of time and space, and wondered why a crowd was peering in at her.

The door was pried open and the man reached over and turned off the ignition. "You all right, Miss?"

Marisa coughed again.

"That's burning rubber. Do you think you can stand?"

Marisa nodded.

An ambulance grated to a halt. The attendant ran up. "Careful, everyone, step back. Can you move your legs?" He shouted above the

259

still screaming siren. He was bending over Marisa, looking into her eyes with an instrument.

She nodded impatiently. "Please. " She stammered to the man who had opened the door. "Please get me out of here?"

The man and the young boy pulled her arms.

"You can't do that." Protested the medic.

Carefully, as not to scratch her on the crushed, jagged metal, they tried to extract her from the wreck.

Her foot caught on the steering wheel.

"Just a minute." The man held her while the boy unlaced and was able to remove her boot. Gently they lifted her out.

"You can put me down, please. I'm not hurt." She insisted. With the topsy-turvy world gone, awareness was restored.

"Let the medics examine you; you should go to the hospital for x-rays."

"No, I'm fine. Please, put me down. See?" She said as he stood her up. She stumbled as a wave of dizziness overtook her, held his arm then took a firm step. "I don't need a hospital."

The man helped her to the rear seat of his four-door sedan. It was an old car, maybe an Oldsmobile; it made no difference. Marisa found, in fact, that she had not been scratched. There were no bruises or blood nor she was not in shock. She was level headed. She looked about for As-Fault while absently giving the local policeman, who had come on the scene, her wallet, telling him her insurance papers and driver's license were inside. She told him she'd arrange to have the wreckage towed away by evening. This was satisfactory to the officer; the Corvette was already off the road and presented no traffic hazard.

As-Fault was nowhere to be seen. The car's four wheels were upended. Marisa marveled how ingenuously the windshield frame was designed and had served so well as a roll-bar. That and the seat belt had kept her head on her shoulders. The cloth top of the convertible was shredded. A fire engine and rescue squad arrived. Still, she did not see her horse. *'For sure, Hamil set this up to keep her away from the show.'* She knew how his mind worked - he assumed, with conviction. that she would wreck the car and chance injury to herself rather than harm As-Fault.

"Please." She asked the man whose car she was in, the man who had pried her out of the wreckage. "Would you take me to Hamil Farm down the road? I'm in a horse show. I must get there right away."

He looked at her as if she were ranting.

She smiled back assuredly.

An excited crowd had gathered around the Corvette. "Did you have anything valuable in the car, Miss? If so, you'd better let me get it out for you. You know how quickly an abandoned wreck is plundered on the roadside, especially an expensive car like this."

"My walking stick, thank-you. I had a black walking stick on the passenger's seat and my bag. Oh! And my boot." She smiled – the 'Southern Belle.'

The boy retrieved them gallantly and the man drove toward Hamil Farm with Marisa in the back seat.

She looked about for Hamil. '*Of course he wasn't there. He was already back at the Farm, satisfied that she was out of his way, injured or dead in the mangled wreck*'. In a fleeting moment of insecurity, she questioned herself what she had seen. '*No, it was not imagined. Hamil was riding As-Fault correct in his premise; she wouldn't run her car into the horse she loved. His arranged mishap had gone awry.*'

Marisa spit granules of glass out of her mouth and brushed her lashes lightly. Tiny flecks sprinkled to her lap and sparkled on the black trousers and black sleeveless t-shirt she had chosen to wear for this long awaited day. She checked her watch. The entire incident had taken ten minutes but with such quasi-slow motion and mind racing fantasies that she was surprised she hadn't lost crucial time. She thanked the man and asked him to let her out of the car at the entrance to the indoor arena.

"I'll drive to the end up here and make a U-turn so you can get out in front. No use you walking any farther than you have to. You're a mighty lucky girl…or foolish."

He drove past the large building and swung around in front of the storage barn where three cats were sleeping in the sun. The site of her humiliation, of self-loathing, of being raped only heightened her anticipation of this final event.

"Is this where you want to go, Miss?"

"Yes, and thanks again." Marisa said getting out of the car, using her cane, not certain if she was, in fact, as able as she expressed.

CHAPTER 17

The glass enclosed observation room attached to the arena now served as the registration office for the Horse Show. Situated as it was, in front of the landfall going down onto the field, its wide window commanded an excellent view of the outdoor activities. Little Rose-Marie had nicknamed it, *'The Playroom'*, because she used to scramble on the small grandstand as a jungle gym while waiting for her father to finish giving lessons.

Marisa bided her time and looked out at the brilliant pageant. It was not yet time to call Ellen. She estimated one hundred high-spirited horses seemingly hot headed and nervous but sweet tempered to those who knew and schooled them. The entrants, adults and children, in their colorful hacking jackets, and fawn colored breeches were making final preparations. They had come distances to participate in what they loved most. Some because they were born to it, others met it and a passion was ignited. From their attire Marisa could read in which class they were entered, and what Hunts were represented. Members of the local Hunt Staff wore the Pink Coats, with magenta and yellow on their collars. Other members wore black jackets.

also with the Hunt colors on their collars. There were many different colored collars as many Hunt clubs were represented. All riders in the show must carry a letter dated within the current year and signed by the Honorary Secretary of the Hunt or by the Master of Foxhounds signifying that they are eligible members. How proudly they strutted. How brightly their tall black boots shone.

Of all those men milling about, or standing in groups, one stood apart. He was wearing his Pink Hunt coat of The Master of the Hounds, however the hunt colors were glaringly absent; only in passing was John Hamil accorded a polite nod of recognition due the host and sponsor of the program.

A warm breeze was blowing the peach blossoms and magnolia petals into a spume of confetti that floated across the pasture and distant fields where tomorrow's Hunt would chase. An earthy smell of horses, and crushed grass mingled with smoking Hickory logs and meat grilling on the barbecue. Already there was a line for hot dogs, burgers and the skewered roasted potatoes that Marisa liked. The mouth-watering aroma caused her stomach to rumble making her aware that she had been up for many hours and hadn't eaten a morsel since last night's dinner. But she wasn't hungry and attributed the complaint to expectancy.

"Excuse me." A young girl said politely; she had been standing next to Marisa at the window. "Could you please help me fasten my hunt cap?" Thin blond pigtails hung down her back. She might have been Rose-Marie, thought Marisa and swallowed the lump in her throat.

"Thanks." The child said and ran off looking like a dressed up doll.

"Good luck. Be careful." Marisa called after her.

It was now crowded inside the office. Marisa looked out the window at the scene where the drama would take place. She hadn't been to Hamil Farm since her fall, nor had she seen any of the Hunt members or fellow students. She recognized Vicky Drake walking down the hill leading her gray horse. She was with her teen-aged daughter, Carrie, who had gained a fine reputation as an equestrian. Each had a white circular placard printed with a bold black number bouncing on her back. The girl had grown so tall. In her hand was a light hunting crop; she was dressed de rigeur: white breeches, a short black silk top hat, black vest and a shad-belly coat. This formal style, commonly called tails or a waist coat, flattered her lean body. From Carrie's outfit, Marisa knew she was entered in the Working Hunter Class. The event was for seasoned amateurs, as well as professional riders, however it is not the rider who is scored; it is the horse that is judged on performance and soundness. A blue ribbon promised accumulated points for the season championship. As-Fault, Marisa believed, was the best of them.

The wall clock said one o'clock. Marisa knew it was late. She imagined Ellen's frustration, torn between staying at the Breakfast to await her call as promised or leaving. She could see the riders studying and memorizing the diagram of the jump course that was just posted at the foot of the judges' stand. She reached in her hand bag for her cell phone…it wasn't there. She felt in her pockets…no phone. '*It must have slipped out when the car turned over,*' She thought and hurried to use the pay phone in the corner.

"I'll just be a moment." The man using the phone laid a handful of coins on the wedge shelf. He smiled with mock sympathy, raising his eyes to the ceiling and continued in the same droning tone. Five minutes passed, still he went on heedless of Marisa's impatient glances.

In a few minutes the Equitation Class would be finished and the ribbons awarded while the jump course was set up for the next program in which As-Fault was entered. She tapped the man on the elbow. "I'm sorry," she said. "It's most important, I have to call the rider for the next event."

Again, he nodded and raised his index finger with no intention of interrupting his conversation. She had counted on using her cellular phone and was not prepared for this delay, which could ruin everything. She couldn't risk Ellen coming 'early.'

"Please." Her voice was menacing.

"One second." He turned back and went on speaking.

Marisa breathed a profanity - snatched the receiver from his hand. "He'll call you back!" She barked, disconnected, then dialed Ellen.

Marisa was at the telephone when Warren walked up the hill toward the barn. He had been looking for her, expecting she would be on the field with Ellen and the other entrants; he saw neither of them. Perhaps, he thought, he had missed her; that she and Ellen were in the barn. '*Strange.*' As-Fault was outside at the bottom of the hill, stepping about nervously, with a stocky man holding his halter. From Marisa's description, Warren knew him to be Benson. But Marisa did not see her husband pass the window; she was looking down, tapping out the seconds against the shelf, waiting for Ellen to come to the phone.

'Finally.'

"Is it time, Marisa? Should I leave now?"

"No, not yet." Marisa tried to keep her voice calm though her heart was beating so fast it was hard to breathe evenly. "They started almost an hour late. I would have called you sooner but the battery on my cell phone didn't hold a charge and the phone here has been tied up.   I won't call you again, the phone here is impossible. The Equitation Class on flat is almost over. You have plenty of time." She said with sincerity, without an iota of truth. "How did the affair go?"

"Marisa, the breakfast was fabulous. After Larry gave his speech I stood next to him on the reception line and all the members of the Rotary Club congratulated me, saying how creative my decorations were." Ellen was glad to hear that she needn't leave in the midst of collecting her kudos. She was looking with pride at the wicker baskets of daisies on each pastel tablecloth and the blinking pin- lights falling as rain drops from the ceiling.

"I'm glad it worked out this way. That's why I don't want you to rush. Enjoy yourself. I bet you look beautiful; I can hear it in your voice."

"I do feel pretty. Larry said I was the best looking woman here. It's better than we planned, now I have more time to stay with him."

Marisa was picturing the Rotarian ladies in their cotton shirtwaist dresses, pearl-buttoned cardigans and practical shoes, some with their white hair tinted blue, all with stomachs, stuffed on the banquet of eggs and grits or turkey sandwiches and potato salad. *'Certainly not my mother's scene. Nor mine.'* She laughed to herself. It might be the only thing they had in common.

Ellen went on speaking, but Marisa wasn't listening; she was watching As-Fault. He was fourth on the line. John Hamil stood arrogantly at his side, unruffled by the horse's straining and rearing or the white froth that already appeared on his neck. Hamil had confidence in As-Fault's staying power and ability. He had trained him.

"I'll have everything ready when you get here, Ellen. Get dressed in As-Fault's stall, the barn will be empty. Look for As-Fault and me on the field. See you later." She hung up hastily and pushed her way past the spectators to the desk where the contestants were registering for their events.

The list for Working Hunter, marked CLOSED, was pinned on the bulletin board behind the counter. Marisa was familiar with many names on the entry list, some of them the finest equestrians and horses on the east coast. *'Ah, there it is,'* Just

as she expected: <u>John Hamil – As-Fault.</u> No
address was given. She smiled so broadly her
cheeks ached. *'The Bastard'.* He had done as his
ego prompted, as she knew he would. In Ellen's
absence, John Hamil had signed himself up to ride
As-Fault. Was she laughing aloud?

Slowly, with her serpentine cane, she made
her way over the soft uneven ground, down the
incline, onto the field where she merged with the
crowd.

Warren stood in the doorway of the open barn; he
saw no one. He looked in the tack room; the bag
with Ellen's clothes was no longer on the peg.
Ellen must have already arrived, changed her cloths
and was on the field. If he kept an eye on As-Fault,
he would surely find Marisa and Ellen together. He
looked once again down the empty aisle of stalls;
satisfied that no one was there he was about to leave
when a huge dog bounded up the ramp and jumped
toward him with excitement. Warren stepped back.

"Dusty, come! Down boy!" A girl stepped
out of one of the stalls near the rear of the barn.
"Hi, Dusty, come here. Good boy, good boy.
Look, I have your ball." She tossed a gnawed ball
that was against the wall into the aisle; Dusty darted
after it. "He just likes to play. He wouldn't hurt
anyone." She said hurriedly while hopping on one
stockinged foot, tugging on a pair of boot hooks to
pull a tall boot over her breeches. She stamped and
yanked, sunk her heel and then fitted the hooks into

the straps of the other boot, pulled it on and sighed. "Ahh." Her hair tumbled in front of her flushed face.

Dusty ran back with the ball in his mouth, dropped it at Warren's feet, and wagged his tail. He picked it up and threw it outside. The dog dashed after it.

The girl turned to Warren. "He'll keep you playing all day, if you let him."

"Ellen?" He asked dubiously. He had never met Ellen. Marisa described her as a retiring figure with never a hair out of place. This girl was not the Plain- Jane he expected to see; this girl was pretty with lively eyes.

"Warren?" She was fidgeting with her stock tie.

He nodded.

"Oh, my gosh, where's Marisa?"

"I thought she'd be with you."

"Did the Working Hunter Class start?"

"I don't think so."

Ellen sighed and stepped back into As-Fault's stall. "It was so sweet of Marisa to give me this gift." She opened the gray box and tried, with nervous, unwilling fingers, to fasten the necklace. "She left it here for me as a surprise."

"Let me help you."

She turned and held up her hair while Warren closed the clasp.

"Marisa will be glad to see you wearing it."

"It's beautiful, but too extravagant; she was doing me a favor to let me ride As-Fault. We're going to win. I'll have the blue ribbon; she should have the necklace."

"You should have seen how happy she was when she was choosing it for you. Wear it."

Ellen hesitated a moment, then touched the necklace appreciatively; she had never had such a lovely piece of jewelry. "Let's go." She grabbed her hunt cap, put an elastic band around her hair and tucked the few stray strands into the bun. "Darn, I can't do this." She said attempting again to knot her stock tie as she ran out the barn door. Warren was behind her. "Marisa will tie it for you on the field."

The diagram of the rugged course for Hunters had been posted and the ten obstacles simulating those found in the hunting field were being set up. There was a natural post fence adorned with roses, a stone wall, a white board fence or gate, a chicken coop and a hedge. There was a water jump adorned with reeds that might have been a stream. Seated high in the the stands were the two judges and next to them, gleaming in the sunlight, the coveted silver Challenge Trophy that would be awarded to the first place winner. The people gathered here were not thrill seekers. They were landed gentry whose interest was in their animals and the ability to achieve that level of finesse, stamina and temperament to chase across the land they loved.

Carrie was the first entrant. She was circling the ring on her Chestnut, 'My Turn.'- a handsome horse with braided mane and tail. The first hurdle was the 'In-and-Out. The horse kicked the last rail, which was only a minor fault, and finished the course at an even hunting pace. The crowd applauded appreciatively. Andrew Reuter was the next rider, looking elegant in his scarlet coat. He rushed the fences but his horse spooked at the hedge when a bird flew up; expertly he was able to settle the horse and urge him over the jump avoiding a refusal which would have eliminated him. Vigorous applause from the crowd.

John Hamil, riding As-Fault, was up next. The entrants on the field stopped checking their tack. The spectators sitting on the hill stood. This was the great John Hamil, the blue ribbon winner, the equestrian of the highest standards, notorious after the newspaper expose' and disgrace of his divorce. They were anxious to see whether his performance would equal his earlier reputation. Many wanted to see him fail - two of whom were condemned to sit in wheel chairs rather than in the saddle.

Marisa was sure Hamil hadn't seen her; he couldn't have because As-Fault would not be quieted and demanded his full attention. But a balking horse was no worry to John Hamil. His face was in repose. Marisa saw that he was content; she could read his mind. He was thinking that she had been badly injured after being forced off the road, and taken away in the show's standby-ambulance. At best, he thought. she had not survived. His plan had succeeded - Marisa Rait was not there. How very fortunate that Ellen Coleman had been delayed leaving As-Fault without a rider. What an unforeseen opportunity this was, and one in which Marisa could not intercede. How clever he was to recognize this chance, with Ellen's absence, to register himself as As-Fault's rider. The Hunt members would behold his brilliant performance riding this exceptional horse. He would be invited back as Master. '*Oh, yes*', Marisa could read his mind.

As-Fault sensed her presence and now stood, well-mannered beside Hamil, who, so pompous, was reveling in the attention given him. Did they expect him to be ruined, not to enter the show he sponsored for lack of a worthy animal? Now was his time to show who was 'The Champion'. After today it would be as before: a full barn of boarders, a full lesson book. Money. And, they would beg him to be Hunt Master. They would beg him.

Clad in black, her hair falling free to her shoulders akin to her horse, Marisa made her way to the fence surrounding the jump course. As-Fault pricked up his ears; his nostrils distended showing crimson. Hamil turned to see what had caught his attention. His eyes met Marisa's; his mouth opened as if to speak then closed, helpless for a moment. Then, he smiled knowing it was too late for anyone to withdraw him as an entrant.

Marisa returned his smile and raised her chin to meet his superior attitude.

274

Suddenly, As-Fault tossed back his head, jerking Hamil's arm upward.

Marisa looked at her feet. Her boots were caked with hard mud; she kicked her foot on the ground to knock it away.

As-Fault stamped the ground.

Hamil mounted and led him into the arena taking the option of doing a circle around to impress the strength and soundness of his mount - his total superiority.

Marisa walked around the fence and stopped opposite the last hurdle, the imposing stack of tree trunks she envisioned in her dreams each night since her fall.

Hamil began the course. No one conformed to the motion of a horse as did John Hamil. Nothing was so well matched as his talent and the powerful black stallion's way of going. They sailed over the tall brush box and pounded to the 'In and Out'. As-Fault eagerly took the jumps with swift grace. All movement of the crowd ceased; all eyes were riveted on the horse and rider. There was no visible signal or change of tempo between them. They were as one – this man and this horse.

Marisa recalled the first time she saw Hamil galloping among the hounds, leading the Hunt…how spellbound she was.

Hamil was standing in the stirrups seemingly weightless. He pulled the horse's head around and swung into the final line of barriers. The stack of tree trunks where Scorpio had slipped - where she had fallen, loomed before him. Marisa was directly in front of them, beyond the fence, and could see Hamil make his approach. As-Fault charged forward at full extension with forging hooves, and mane rippling behind him.

It was the finale of a perfect run.

'Remember, remember,' Marisa breathed unspoken words to her horse. *'Ignore the spurs, remember this man, his smell, the pain of poles crashing into your chest, remember. Watch me, As-Fault, watch me.'*

She knew he saw her.

Hamil was tucked forward, compelling As-Fault to the barrier. Faster…faster.

Marisa turned her back and began walking from the field.

Halfway up the hill, she came face to face with Ellen. Marisa saw her mouth drop open in shock, saw two hands go to her head as she joined the horrified cry of all who witnessed As-Fault refuse the jump.

He stopped.

John Hamil was hurled headlong over the barrier. Marisa heard the thud as his body struck the ground. She turned. From her height on the crest of the hill, she could see the man sprawled on the ground, against the tree trunks. His scarlet coat was covered with mud; his head, in an unnatural and undignified position, was peering unseeingly too far over his left shoulder; a thin line of blood trickled from his nose.

The ambulance, always held in abeyance during such shows, was unable to drive onto the field. It was reported that it had been called away to a previous accident involving a red Corvette and when it returned it had gotten stuck in the ruts dug by the traffic along the driveway. There it remained. The driver and the intern, himself a student of the former champion, rushed down the hill to Hamil's side. Carefully, they lifted the limp form onto the stretcher, carried it through the crowd, up the hill passing Marisa on the way to the ambulance. The stretcher was slid inside; the door slammed shut.

Marisa let her walking stick slide into the grass.

The heavyset Judge, whom Maria remembered from her first class, led As-Fault off the field. She barely noticed Warren, who was standing beside Ellen.

A child screamed. It was the little blond girl whose Hunt Cap she had fastened earlier.

Her father was by her side. "It's not a real snake," He laughed picking up the serpentine cane. "Someone must have dropped it. Nothing to be afraid of. Here, walk with it up the hill."

Inside the ambulance the young doctor examined his patient. The pulse was weak and there were no reflexes. "His neck is broken." He stated, matter-of-factly, while raising one of the eyelids in the ashen face.

The driver said. "He's a dead man unless we get him to surgery in a few minutes."

The intern covered the still man with a white sheet. "Nice boots, huh?"

"Seems a waste, at the hospital they'll cut 'em off."

"Umm." The intern muttered. "Look like my size. Come on, give me a hand."

"I'll hold him. You pull"

The Judge brought As-Fault up to Ellen and told her to put him in her van. Ellen was too dumbstruck to move. In that instant her face had lost all color, the muscles sagged, and she looked, to Marisa, like melting Vanilla ice-cream with a round cherry painted mouth which opened and screamed soundlessly. Marisa thanked the Judge and loaded As-Fault into the trailer. Warren took Ellen's elbow and Marisa removed her hunt cap. It was then that she saw the necklace. Warren saw her eyes open wide in recognition; her eyebrows came together in a frown of inquiry. She looked up at him - whispered. 'Were? How did she get that?'

Warren put his finger to his lips. "Shh, you promised. No more talk."

"But…"

Warren shook his head and Marisa knew better than to proceed.

She buckled Ellen into the back seat and sat beside Warren.

Warren drove past the ambulance still not excavated from the mud. The wheels spun. digging deeper and deeper into the rut. In the rear view mirror, Marisa watched the revolving red light get smaller as they drove away from Hamil Farm. She looked at the golden weathervane on the turret of the barn for the last time. Ellen, whose eyes were closed, was gripping the gold chain at her throat. The siren of the ambulance continued to wail.

It was over, a justified ending. She touched her husband's hand. He pressed her fingers to his lips.

Warren and Marisa would have their baby.